Self. Centered.

An Interactive Novel

Memory is the protagonist of our lives.

Personal reflection as a means to connection.

By Shayndel Plotkin

ISBN-13: 978-1495280573

ISBN-10: 1495280578

ABOUT SHAYNDEL PLOTKIN

Mrs. Shayndel Plotkin has been an educator and writer for more than 20 years. As a young woman, Shayndel was hired by Charles Bronfman and the CRB Foundation to pilot an Israel Experience task force in Palm Beach County, Florida, in order to explore the impact visiting Israel would have on young Jewish people (including herself). This project later became known as Birthright Israel.

As a staff writer for the Sun-Sentinel and the Jewish Journal, Shayndel had the privilege of becoming well-versed in the many non-profit organizations and philanthropies in the South Florida area. Through her journalistic abilities she was able to raise awareness and funds for underprivileged Jewish immigrants and Jewish youth in the area. As a writer and memoirist, Shayndel has been hired to write several family histories and has been the ghost writer of two memoirs for philanthropists in South Florida and Israel.

As an educator, Shayndel continues to teach and guide children and adults of all ages through her classes, articles and, most importantly, at her Shabbos table.

Shayndel is married to Rabbi Baruch Plotkin and together they have precious children growing in Jewish values and love of Torah and God.

With humility and kavod, may the Almighty shine upon us His greatest blessings.

iv

This book is dedicated to Shoshanna Rachel Bat HaRav EliMelech.

Her journey here was far too short but her memory and legacy live on forever. In her merit, may all of our mothers, sisters, and daughters embody the wisdom of the righteous women of the ages.

www.shoshiestern.com

Acknowledgments

I humbly show my gratitude to God, the Almighty, for allowing my voice to be found. This novel has been a process of journaling my personal story while staying true to the fictionalized character, Hannah, as she embarks on her own journey created on the pages that follow.

Thank you to my husband for caring for our children while I quietly snuck away and found the time to complete this work. His support and belief in my voice enabled me to push myself in a way that has been necessary for my growth, my truth and my enlightenment.

Thank you to my oldest son, Binyomin Aryeh. One day he smiled at me and said, "Ima, it makes me so happy to see you doing what you love to do."

I love you, my souls, for filling me up with so much love and showing me how much I am capable of giving. For without you, I would have never known that through giving I am always receiving.

Professional Acknowledgments

I would like to extend further acknowledgment to the following professionals who helped me accomplish this endeavor:

Andrew Blitman, a friend, student, and teacher. Thank you for your expert layout, design, and editorial supervision. Rivka Estrin, you are an amazing woman and I am so blessed to have you as a dear friend, mentor, and editor. Glen Hoffman, thank you for your graphic art and formatting, and to you and your family for our growing friendship. Gloria Frydlewski, thank you for bringing Hannah Slone to life through your cover art. Rebbetzin Tamar Meth, Gwen Weinberger, Deena S. Borzak and the Stern family, you are truly special friends and I adore your insights and advice.

Foreword: My Holiest Experience

I stood at the Western Wall (Kotel), at first, from a distance. I walked toward it blindly, knowing neither its history nor its significance. How good it was to be there.

A warm, familiar energy—not the summer heat— emanated from the sacred site. Although it was my first visit, I felt as though I had been there before.

Slowly I approached the Wall, the last remnant of Solomon's Temple. Before I could pray, I was stopped by an older man. He handed me a shawl to cover my tank top and shorts, clothing too casual for such a holy place. I put it on as he requested. As the immense stone Wall loomed in front of me, I began to meditate to God.

My hands cradled two notes with well-wishes for the people I loved—one for myself and my family, the other for my Bubby, grandmother, in heaven. I gently, anonymously, inserted them into a wall-crack.

Although I was nervous, I noticed how my written supplications joined the millions of paper prayers in the Kotel's cracks. Then I took a few steps forward. My toes almost touching the Wall, I focused on my meditations. I felt as if God himself was watching me.

As I prayed silently, I closed my eyes. The top of my head rested reverently on the bricks. My mind drifted gracefully, my thoughts turned inward.

When my eyes opened, I found myself in a peaceful and safe place. With great praise, I read aloud the Tehillim (Psalms) from my Bat Mitzvah Siddur, a gift from my uncle years before.

A torrent of bittersweet tears fell from my eye, each drop rippling down my face. I stood against the Wall and looked up. The Kotel's sacred energy flowed through me.

As I began to comprehend my religion, I realized how great it was—and how proud I was—to be Jewish.

Later that day, I called my mother and told her about my epiphany. Upon my admission, she, coincidentally, admitted how earlier in the day she had some strange visions of me. "You were crying but you were happy", my Mom said. "The feeling was so strong that I started crying, too."

Upon further discussion, we discovered that our experiences were connected…right down to the timing. They happened simultaneously, as if by divine providence.

For the first time in a long time, I felt a close bond with my Mom and to the Almighty, He was greater than both of us.

How to Use This Book

First and foremost please enjoy this book as a novel. Embark with Hannah along her personal awakening and her journey. I hope you grow with her as she explores her faith and her destiny.

Not only did I write this book as an exploration of this one woman's search, but I also tried to use it as a tool for my own journey and my many moments in life. The writing prompts and prayers along Hannah's road are also intended for the reader to use as a springboard for personal reflection.

Personal Reflection as a means to Connection.

As you read, you may want to invest some time in your own thoughts and contemplations. Often times, when I read a book and I really connect with the protagonist, I wonder: What would I have done in her situation? Where would I have gone? What would I have said?

Reading is a sacred space where the fast pace of time slows down. I hope you find the space and pace to use this book in a way that inspires you.

Table of Contents

I. The Key

"**Master of the world, behold! I cast my prayer before You. For the key of life is in Your hand, and You have not transferred it to an agent.**"

"Please, take the key, Hannah."

"No. I am afraid. I want you to come with me."

"No. I can't," said her Father. "I must stay here and repair – rebuild," he added. "Can you reach out and grab it and then run, Hannah, run as far away as you can? Don't look back."

"I can't see it!" I cried. Hannah reached for it and felt its sharp edges. Through the smoke and flames she could almost see the shining metal, but it was too clouded and dark. "The fire is too strong. I am sorry, Father. I can't reach it. It was not meant for me. I am not the one who is meant to take it from you."

"Run, then. Run, Hannah. The fire is burning everything. It will not stop. We are being destroyed."

"Please let me be the one to reach for the key. Let me be the one," I begged.

I woke up confused and uncertain if I was, in fact, dreaming.

Have you ever had a dream that stuck with you for the rest of the day?

> **Blessed are You, God, our God, King of the universe, Who removes sleep from my eyes and slumber from my eyelids.**

I awoke, shaken a bit and I felt disturbed and still tired. My eyes squinted due to the sun beaming in to greet me through my small studio apartment window on the Upper West Side of Manhattan. It was the only window in the tiny 200-square-foot room I called home. I couldn't shake the feeling that something was different. But what?

Today would not be like any other day. I knew something was about to happen that would change my life. I often thought something special would happen to me. I lived in a bit of a "dreamer" state of mind all the time. People often thought I was daydreaming.

As a journalist for the past six years, I was always witnessing strange and exciting things. But always from a distance; I was always an observer.

Today, as I replayed the dream in my mind, I had an eerie feeling that I might be the one being observed. I would be the one having the experience that would change the course of my life… forever.

Right now, though, I could barely get out of bed.

I was still hazy from the last moments of a less-than-sound sleep, so I tossed the covers off and moved slowly and methodically to the other side of the bed. I would always move toward the nightstand where I kept my glasses and prayer book. Mostly I kept the prayer book there for comfort and warmth.

It was my anchor to her tumultuous past. It gave me a stronghold on something I barely understood, but knew I needed in order to keep a steady course in life and have my feet firmly planted on the ground.

First came a deep breath. Another immediately followed. I slowly inched my way to the bedside table and took my glasses, accidentally knocking the prayer book from its place. It fell to the floor. I quickly grabbed it and with a kiss upon its cover, gazed at it. I kept it at my bedside, but never really looked inside. It was old and tattered, faded and worn. It was an heirloom. So it was important.

This prayer book was a gift from my Bubby, 20 years before. I thought about where this holy book had traveled. What it had seen. Who's eyes had looked upon its words for comfort and peace? Bubby used it, every day. Bubby had a long journey, I knew, with a past unknown to me but pieced together only through broken English and Yiddish and stories of the old country, people and places so distant and forgotten. I always felt it was impossible to know where Bubby actually came from. Too many made-up stories told to me as a child. I caressed the cover.

Although I grew up in a Jewish home, I never felt totally connected to my roots. I went to a Jewish day school in Brooklyn and on Shabbos my family would attend a small shul down the street from my home on Avenue J. my father was close with the Rabbi but I rarely noticed him or the other adults in the quiet, murmuring room of supplicants.

While I sat on my bed I began to think about Bubby. Suddenly the memories of my first time at the Kotel, the Western Wall, six years ago, with Bubby on my mind and the very first prayers I had ever really said to God came back to me.

Since then, I had been saying that specific prayer every day, well, almost every day. Although I did not consider myself religious at this time in my life, I felt a yearning to connect to that time in Israel as often as I could. It gave my soul a certain centering and my body a peaceful state of mind.

The prayer was taken from the morning prayer service...

> **"...draw our scattered ones near from among the nations and bring in our dispersions from the ends of the earth. Bring us to Zion, Your city, in glad song, and to Jerusalem, home of Your sanctuary, in eternal joy to observe Your decrees and to do Your will, wholeheartedly."**

"The Morning Ritual"

I began my morning ritual. After the one prayer, I would stretch and get up. Walk toward the shower. Stop and look in the mirror. Continue on. But, today, instead of walking into the bathroom, I returned to the bedside table and opened the book.

I saw the Mode Ani prayer, a sweet thank you to God. Thank you. I can do that, I thought and began to recite the prayer. First in English and then, the Hebrew.

I tried to focus on His great blessings and not on all the things I usually worried about. All the missed opportunities that I let slip away. Now 26, single and living in NYC. I tried to forget the dream and restless sleep I had just had.

"Focus," I told myself. Focus will bring clarity and connection. And Mode Ani came to me with a clear message - like I was unlocking a treasure with the *key* I was trying to reach. I recited it at my bedside, quietly at first and then louder and with certainty. I felt that I was calming down now. Unlike a workout at the gym that exhausted my body but not my mind, this relaxed me completely.

> **"I gratefully thank You, O living and Eternal King. For You have returned my soul within me with compassion – abundant is Your faithfulness."**

"Returned my soul?" I meditated on the words. Today. I am grateful for today. For right now. For the moment I have. The dream. Turn over the key to me? Return my soul to me? Hmmm? Was there a connection?

I washed and continued with my ritual. I felt energized this morning - a different energy than usual. I felt a desire to do something. But what? For the past several months I had felt a stirring, unsettling, like I was preparing for something.

Yet, sometimes I felt exhausted. Lost. Even though I had a job I loved. A job I had dreamed of having for as long as I could remember. I left my family, my community and the world where I grew up behind me. I had to. My parents would have never let me pursue journalism. They believed I would forget all I had learned as a child. That I would stop keeping Shabbos and being Kosher. They were right. They worried who I would marry?

After all, Miriam was happily married. Miriam was Orthodox. Miriam was pregnant. They never asked if I was happy.

Was I... happy? Am I lost?

For the past few months Hannah walked slower, ate slower, dressed slower and moved about basically... slower. Like I was in a haze. Like I was in a daze.

Today. It was as if I was filled with a new lease on life.

It had been a hard few years. Dating and never meeting the right guy. Watching my friends get married and have children. I was so happy for them, but becoming more and more depressed about my own life. It seemed to be taking me so many years to meet Mr. Right.

The waiting. The times when I had given up. The days when I felt lost and alone.

Meeting Mr. Wrong, Again...

It was a rainy day in November, the City was grayish in color. The buildings, the streets, the sky. It was similar to many days in the City. I was to meet a friend in midtown for lunch and as I arrived at the restaurant she I noticed I was stepping on a rainbow. It was bright and colorful yet, to me, it looked sad. The aftermath of a dreary night.

Everything looked sad these days, especially after the night I would now have to relay to my happily married friend, with two children. I entered, ready to tell the tale. Why did she, her "friend," want to hear the gossip of a bad date? Did she get pleasure from a friends' pain?

Did she feel better about her life? Was it reassuring that she was doing everything right and I was doing everything wrong? Have I done that to others or to myself? Have I done something wrong?

Hannah is feeling alone these days. Things in her life are not going as she had hoped. Do you ever have days or moments when you feel alone? How do you get through them?

Recounting a "J" Date

The tale went like this: The night before was yet another unsuccessful JDate. This one, like the others, ended for her before it even began. The guy was incapable of having a conversation that had to do with anything meaningful. He kept talking about his job as a stock broker and *this* deal and investing *this* time and in *this* way and so on.

I told him that I don't invest but that didn't seem to matter because he was absolutely fine talking to himself about himself for a solid two and a half hours. I got home late and fell asleep drained and alone. Hating myself and my life. Like I was dropped somewhere in a dark pit. A cave in the middle of nowhere and I could not escape.

Where would my salvation come from? Who would find me and save me from this lonely existence? Why was I put here? On this planet, in this city.

The morning was getting away from me so I stepped it up a bit. I looked in the mirror again. This time dressed and ready for the day. "I am happy. I know things will fall into place."

As I stared at my reflection, a new ease and peace filled me up.

Contentment. Satisfaction. Fulfillment. Trust. That God knows who I am and what is best for me. Today and always.

About 20 minutes later, now with a new ritual behind me, I emerged from my room ready to take a look at my busy schedule.

I took a look at the calendar and couldn't help thinking about that dream. What key? I remember what it looked like. It was all so vivid. How can I have such vivid dreams without even having a restful night's sleep?

A precious key would be given to me? What did I have to do with it? How will I get it? What will it unlock?

What does it mean to trust in God?

II. A Rainbow's Got My Back

Taking far too long to choose the right outfit and comfortable shoes, I exited her high-rise apartment in the City and hailed a cab.

Before I entered the back seat, I stepped on a dewy, post-rain-shower rainbow. I love rainbows. Rainbows are always so connecting. They disappear into the empty spaces and remind us of even our most hidden connections with the world around us.

"Please take me to 55th and Central Park West." Just a few blocks from my apartment but in the rain it would have felt like forever. Plus I was so excited today. I was seeing Rivka a.k.a. Rebbeca. She was now using her new and improved Hebrew name. Seeing her for the first time in two years. Eagerness and joy raced through my body.

Anxious, I quickened my pace as I paid the fare and ran toward the door of the restaurant. A new restaurant, one I hadn't been to before. Kosher. With a giggle about my friend who had left New York two years earlier and had written that she found her spiritual self in (no other place than) Israel. She now only ate kosher.

Cool, I thought, as I entered. It smelled good and looked clean. Kippot, yarmulkas, everywhere. I suddenly felt holier myself. It isn't like it's totally foreign to me, I mean, I did eat kosher as a kid, "kind of".

"Hannah!" I heard my name and turned toward the door. Rebecca. Rivka? I could not believe my eyes. Before me stood this woman in what looked like a turban on her head covering all of her hair and a belly. A pregnant belly. But not only did she look different. Next to her was a boy with long, dark, curly hair covering his eyes. He was clinging to her long skirt which was draped to her feet.

We hugged and I felt so strange. A bit foreign, in a place I had once known so well. We started talking and it was as if no time had passed. We laughed like before about the silliest moments we had had growing up. She was always the daredevil of the group. A risk-taker. Rebel. She told me she was just visiting family for a few weeks and would be returning to Israel where she lived and where he husband was studying to become a rabbi.

"You're married to a rabbi," I asked laughing, but in a good way.

"I would love you to meet him. Maybe you can come for a visit," she said, genuinely interested.

"Maybe."

"I know you, when you say maybe it means you won't even consider it."

"Not true," I said.

We continued reminiscing for a while and I knew, sadly, I would have to leave. We shared a pizza and fries as always. Then I gave her a tight and clingy hug and said goodbye. Yosef gave me a kiss on the cheek. I felt his unconditional love.

"L'Hitraot, (bye)," she shouted back as she darted for a cab. As she got into her cab with Yosef, I noticed she dropped her keys on the curb.

"Rivka!" I shouted. "Rivka! Wait!"

But the cab drove off. I looked for her number and couldn't find it at the moment. Shoot! I have to head to work. Like right now!

Focus, I told myself. I have a big story to do this week. She will be in touch as soon as she realizes she has no keys.

I was glad I hadn't shared my dream with her. Not like that, so quickly and flaky. I also didn't get to tell her I was leaving. Nobody knew yet.

Nobody knew how important this day was to me. That this would be my final farewell to the paper where I had worked for the last 7 years.

As a staff writer for the New Yorker, I had never missed a deadline and I didn't want my last few weeks to be remembered for one of the three cardinal sins. Missing a deadline or sharing an opinion or leading an interview.

Although I loved the job more than anything, I felt that it was time to move on.

Move on, yes. But to what? Where was I going? What was I going to do next?

I was longing for something. Yearning for something new.

Searching. Like I lost something and now needed to find out what it was. When I described this to friends and co-workers I would use the word "adventure." I was tired of writing about someone else's adventures. I wanted to have my own. I guess I am a daydreamer, I thought.

But I knew something deeper was going on. So I made a decision and was going to stick to it. I was scared out of my mind. But I was 26 and not sure where my life was heading. It was time to take a hard look at who I was and what I wanted from myself.

Hannah yearns for change/deeper meaning in her life. Have you ever longed for something deeper but had no idea how to find it? What did you do to make that dream a reality?

_____
_____
_____
_____
_____
_____
_____
_____
_____
_____
_____
_____
_____
_____
_____
_____
_____
_____
_____
_____
_____
_____
_____
_____
_____
_____
_____
_____
_____

At least the sun was out. I dropped the keys in my oversized bag and hurried toward the office. The street was dry, as though the rain was just a dream. Had I seen a rainbow? Had I had a dream?

I walked the few blocks to the New Yorker. Trying to get my head focused for the day ahead. I was working on a big story. I was scheduled to meet with the head rabbi of the Brooklyn Jewish Center. A place I knew well. I had grown up right there. I had been there each week as a young girl.

But it was also a place I had left behind. I left it, the neighborhood, and all that I knew as a child, in order to grow up and find my way, on my own. It led me away from a lot of the Jewish culture and practice of my past. Returning to the Center, now, at a time of distress for the community was hard. Seeing the site burned to the ground was going to be a shock.

The Center had burned down months ago in what had been called a hate crime, by all the reporters. The crazy thing was that when they found the presumed perpetrator and wanted to convict, the rabbi refused to do so. The other community leaders got together, even the non-Jews, and tried to force the conviction. But the rabbi remained silent. He would not point the man out in a lineup and the case was dropped. Rabbi Marcus has not granted an interview with anyone since, nor has he spoken about the crime publically.

After clearing the land, they had decided to rebuild the Center in its exact location. But the rabbi, Rabbi Avraham Marcus, was holding up the construction. He was refusing to rebuild. He received grants and city funds, but because his name was on the lease they could not move forward without him.

With the land cleared, the city permits were ready and the only thing holding up the rebuild was this rabbi. The groundbreaking was planned for two weeks from today. I was supposed to find out the real story behind the rabbi's decision not to convict the supposed criminal or give the OK to start construction.

This Center was the heartbeat of the Jewish community in Brooklyn. It was the primary source of inspiration and education for the children and adults.

So many people had come out to support it. On the other side there was Rabbi Marcus, strong-willed and silent.

He said he was concerned for Jews to gather like that, in public. He didn't say more. My editor was surprised that he had agreed to be interviewed at this time - and by me, a woman. My editor thought that Orthodox men couldn't talk to women.

But the rabbi specified that he would only talk to Miss Hannah Slone. I don't really know him well. Did he remember me from when I was a young girl, growing up down the street?

Maybe he had seen my articles? That felt good for my ego!

As I pondered the terrible crime, I didn't understand why this rabbi was so against the building project, especially now that the criminal had been convicted. Even I am upset and angry by these types of crimes and the violence. And I am not even religious.

What was his problem? Did it have something to do with the costs involved - both financial and communal? Had the goals of the Center changed? Did he not care anymore about the community?

As those thoughts penetrated my mind, I started getting pumped and excited to write the story. Not only was it a juicy article, but I had a bit of a personal interest. I had grown up there, after all. I did not, however, share this with my editor. I had a personal bias. So unprofessional, I know.

But secretly, lately, I had longed for an excuse to go back and see the neighborhood. Even though my parents, sister and brother-in-law still live there, I always insist that they visit me in the city. I feel disconnected to that place. I usually don't even miss it. But lately, something in me was aching to go back. **To return.**

Hannah realizes she needs to return to her roots as a way to discover who she truly is. Have you strayed from your past and, if so, have you or would you want to return?

I decided to walk the 22 blocks to work. A few blocks in I realized I forgot to return Miriam's call. She always wanted to hear from me at various check points throughout the day.

It rang. No answer. I hung up and continued to walk, now 16 blocks to go.

I caught a glimpse of my reflection in the bus stop window. I always feel that I am 10 pounds heavier than I should be. Than I should be? Based on whose standards? My own? Television? Magazines? Men? I dress fine. Conservative, one might say. But pretty.

Ring, ring... "Hey. Hi, sorry I missed the call my cell was on vibrate."

"Oh, OK sis," I said quickly and with a tone of annoyance in my voice.

"Everything is great," she continued. "The baby is right on schedule and positioned in the right place. We are going to have a baby sooner than later!" she shouted with a loud enthusiasm.

"My sister is having a baby!" I screamed, trying to sound excited. Miriam had no hesitation in her voice, no concern or questions about abilities as a mother. It was as if she always had the key, the knowledge and faith that she would be fine.

On the other hand, I have been thinking and contemplating everything in my life. I can't even make a decision about what to wear without sweating.

My sister was destined for motherhood all her life. She has always been calm and clear in her decisions. I have been destined for a life of self-doubt and deliberation.

I thought of the rainbow, disappearing into nowhere. Like self-doubt, it gets you nowhere. Yet, with having faith, you are left with a feeling that you're not alone and that God has your back.

"Hello?" asked Miriam. "Are you still there? You always go off talking on a tangent."

"Oh, sorry," I said. "I am so happy for you and I can't wait until the weekend to see you all. Give my love to Ben. Bye." I hung up. I continued walking and stepped on another rainbow. A rainbow is supposed to remind us of the covenant between God and the Jewish people. (I still remembered some things from Hebrew School.)

Hannah remembers the story of Noah and how the rainbow is the symbol of God's covenant with man. When she sees a rainbow, she feels reassured by its presence. What symbols strengthen your faith in yourself and the world?

III.   Back to Brooklyn

The weekend will be great, I thought. Seeing my parents and spending time with family. It is always terrific. Until they start in on the boyfriend questions. My father is always quick to make a suggestion about my appearance or my career choices.

I know he means well, and mostly, his comments feel reassuring and comforting. But sometimes his certainty is just like a bull-dozer. "Do this and this and you will be just fine. Done." Like a bulldozer, he doesn't look at me as a whole person, just like a building, a three-dimensional structure, just aim and fire. I am the mark so bulldoze me and if I collapse he can just rebuild me?

Sometimes I pray, "Please, God, help me to stand on my own two feet firmly planted on the ground."

I arrived at work energized and with my creative journalistic juices already flowing. I had just enough time to meet with my editor for some final notes on the goal of the story and review my logistics.

I didn't want him to know my personal stakes in this community center. Although he knew I was Jewish, I had never truly been connected to one community so strongly. I had never let my personal view or feelings skew a story or interfere with journalism. I wouldn't now.

Even though I may have disappeared from home and am not religious, I still try my best to stay true to my convictions. Sometimes I fall short of what I believe is right. But doesn't everyone?

Hannah is struggling to stay true to her convictions. Has there been a time when a truth has separated you from others? What was that truth and how did you bridge the gap?

_____
_____
_____
_____
_____
_____
_____
_____
_____
_____
_____
_____
_____
_____
_____
_____
_____
_____
_____
_____
_____
_____
_____
_____
_____
_____
_____
_____
_____

I grabbed my notepad and headed into Joe Baker's office, and we began our usual interplay of ideas and demands and word count and space issues for the story.

"So Hannah, this story is really important for the paper, you know that."

"Of course." I reassured him. "I have it covered. I am heading there right now and I am not coming back until I get the whole story and the rabbi's assurance that he will be at the groundbreaking for the Center, standing next to you and the Mayor."

I walked out feeling nervous and tried to toughen up for the next meeting.

I felt ready to head to the meeting site, first to the Rabbi's home to meet with him. Then together we'd walk over to view the land. Today he would share the importance of the original Center and recount the crime.

He was in the building when the crime was committed and he lost more than the structure. He lost a sense of the security and the ability for the Center to continue its work. I couldn't imagine his feeling of loss.

Have you ever experienced insurmountable loss? If so, how do you cope with it? If not, how would you help a friend and/or relative who has experienced such sorrow?

I hailed a cab and jotted some notes on the ride
over. Over the bridge and then to the rabbi's home. It was
a small structure alongside the shul, on Ocean Parkway. I
had remembered it from my childhood. I hadn't been back
to this area of Brooklyn in so long.

The nostalgia poured all over me like a warm bowl
of chicken soup, (just the broth). I felt both comforted and
guilty. I walked up the stoop and knocked. Once, twice and
at the third knock, a deep voice from behind the heavy
wooden frame called out, "Zaide, it's the lady from the
news."

Lady? When did I become that lady? I was just a
girl playing hopscotch and jacks down the street from here.
My father taught me how to play stoopball here. But this
was no longer a place I called home. It was a foreign world

now. I was a stranger here. How can I feel so warm and familiar yet at the same time feel lost and different?

Have you ever felt like a stranger in a place unknown or unfamiliar? Have you ever felt like a stranger to yourself?

The door opened. I was ushered in to the Rabbi's study. The hallway was narrow and lined with bookshelves. The books were all Hebrew and intimidating. My third-grade Hebrew education certainly could not decipher one from the next. I could barely fit through the awkward path.

I walked sideways, led by this man with long curls and a face of purity and kindness. He knocked once and entered. He walked over to the frail man at the end of the room. He gave him a warm embrace and a kiss upon his cheek. Without a look back he left the room and almost shut the door, leaving it a bit ajar.

I sat near a desk overflowing with papers and books. Photographs and history. The smell in the air was that of musty pages and old leather. There was a dim light and the furniture was dark and worn. I sat comfortably, though, pen in hand and ready to hear the words of the rabbi.

IV.   A Burning Vision

After a few awkward minutes of silence. "Oye Vey, I can't find my key," a low voice mumbled. "Excuse me, sir?" I said. Also in a lower tone than usual. Maybe he hadn't seen me or made the connection that I was sitting in his study.

"I can't believe it, the day we are supposed to talk about the Center and go over to the building site and I can't find the key to the lock box. It has all the contracts and documents for the building. It is the only key to the box. The master key, they call it."

My cyes scanned the catastrophically disorganized room. I wanted to offer to help, but, what a mess. Before I could question my decision he gave a sigh and sat at the desk. I could barely see his face above the stacks of papers. I noticed the Yiddish, the Hebrew and the English pages mixed together.

"It doesn't matter anyway. I guess it is not meant to be. Let's begin," he said.

I agreed with a quick nod and took out a pen. "Great, so, please tell me the facts that lead up to the fire. What was happening here in the neighborhood to cause such a terrible event? What is the anti-Semitism like here? It must be so tense and there must be problems with Jews and others all the time." I felt like I was leading the conversation but he was silent and I had to get the ball rolling.

There was a moment of silence.

"Shhhh. Please, kinder, child, let me talk a bissle and you, you'll listen." Just then, the man with the curls walked in with two glasses of water, one for the rabbi and one for me. His was accompanied by two small blue pills.

I wondered, but turned away. I didn't want him to feel uncomfortable that I was watching his every move.

Like I was invading his private space.

Hannah feels uncomfortable as she notices the pills the rabbi must take. Have you ever felt your privacy had been violated or that you violated the privacy of someone else?

_____
_____
_____
_____
_____
_____
_____
_____
_____
_____
_____
_____
_____
_____
_____
_____
_____
_____
_____
_____
_____
_____
_____
_____
_____
_____
_____
_____

"Now, I will begin telling you about the..." he paused... "terrible fire". "It was more than I could bear. I remember the heat and the flames. I stood still for a while until the smoke penetrated the room. It was so heavily filling the room that I had to drop to my knees and crawl to the window. I was in a small study on the second floor, just across from the Beit Midrash (study hall)."

I listened carefully, keenly aware of the sweat building upon his forehead. His eyes filled with tears as if the smoke was piercing him right now.

"It was a terrible night."

"It happened at night?" I clarified.

"Evening, after Maariv, the evening prayers. We were supposed to have a night seder, a night of learning. No one had arrived yet so I was preparing for the class in my study. I heard a crash and then I ran to the door where I saw this ball of fire growing, glowing downstairs. I stood silent and froze, in shock."

"Did you call for help?" I asked.

"I didn't call the fire department or the police. Someone else must have done so. I just stood and then the choking smoke and the thick graying air surrounded me. I heard the fire trucks coming closer and fell to the floor. I crawled and then, I don't remember what happened next. I woke up in the hospital."

He was finished recounting the memory, I could tell. But we hadn't yet gotten to the reason this fire was all over the news for two weeks. He wasn't ready to talk about what he hadn't done.

I wondered if I should go on. Should I probe into a sacred place that wasn't open for me? I am a journalist; I am encouraged and reminded myself. These are the hard questions. These are the questions that bring about change. Then, as if he heard my secret thoughts...

"Questions? The right ones at the right time are valuable. Even life-changing. But one must be ready for that change. If not, they are just questions left lingering in the air."

"What happens to them?" I asked, hearing myself sound like a child, eyes wide open, waiting for the secret to be revealed. "The answers will come. But only at the right time," he concluded.

"The night was cold and the fire was burning the Center. The core of our community was going up in flames.

This place with its holiness and power. This was not only a place of prayer and community, where we held simchas, like Bar Mitzvahs and Bat Mitzvahs, weddings and L'Chaims, it was also a place that kept our most sacred, most precious possessions."

"Your holy books?" I inquired.

"Books? Books can be replaced," said the rabbi, emphatically. "Souls cannot."

"This was where our children learned Torah. It was a space. A time that we could set apart, aside from the rest of the week, and engage in holy study."

"The Center was the place we built to care for our little neshamas, souls. All those holiest neshamas. Our children and grandchildren. They destroyed our space. Our space to get close to... God". His voice trailed off as if a wind had swept through and carried his words away.

I remember my childhood. It brings a smile to my face when I think about a safe space I had. How do you feel about your childhood? Do you recount your childhood days with fondness or spite? How was your life influenced by those experiences and/or your perceptions of them?

_____
_____
_____
_____
_____
_____

He took a sip of his water. So did I.

"You are planning to rebuild? That is why I am here? Right, Rabbi."

"They burned the Center. The core. That's it."

"Gurnisht," he said, sounding exasperated. "Why to rebuild? For what?" It is not the time to rebuild now. It is not my job. I am not the one to rebuild it. It burned down while I was here. It burned down from the pain that surrounds us in our very neighborhood." Then he got very, very silent.

"That awful fire," he continued.

"Yes, I know," I said.

"No, not the one here in Brooklyn. The one in Poland. The one in Lublin. The one in Krakow. The one in... the one in Jerusalem. It was an inferno. It burned for so many days and nights."

"But it was out in a few hours, wasn't it? Rabbi? Wasn't the fire out in a few hours? The firemen were even able to save some books and the Torah," I confirmed.

"They couldn't put it out. They can never put it out."

I saw he was getting so worked up and I was getting scared and concerned for his health. Should I get the grandson? His wife?

"I understand how upset you are," I said. "Then why didn't you want to press charges against the guy that did it? That would have been justice."

"So what? Why? If not him, then it would have been someone else. We destroy. We rebuild. And we will destroy again."

"Like the Bet HaMikdash, the Holy Temple." His voice was stronger now. I could hear the quiver of rage.

Have you ever built something that was destroyed beyond repair? How did you cope with the loss? Did you rebuild?

_____
_____
_____
_____
_____
_____
_____
_____
_____
_____
_____
_____
_____
_____
_____
_____
_____
_____
_____
_____
_____
_____
_____
_____
_____
_____
_____
_____

I tried to direct the interview back to the topic. "I am so sorry, Rabbi. I can't imagine how horrible this has been for your family and your community. The pain and loss. I'm so sorry. I'm so sorry." I caught myself saying the same sentence over and over.

"They did put away the person who did this. But it wasn't him alone. He was a symbol of the hate and anger that we have going on here. One person did not do this," he said. "Many people, many different people did this. So much hate. So many confused and angry souls. We all did this. Jews, non-Jews, whites and blacks. Religious and non-religious."

"So, you're saying, I am one of the people responsible, too?" I asked. "How can you say this person was not to blame - That he was confused? He wasn't confused, Rabbi. He knew exactly what he was doing. He was burning down a shul," I said loudly.

Listen to me, I thought to myself. Calm down. This isn't your fight. This isn't your right. A journalist doesn't get emotional. She gets the facts.

I was getting angry and about ready to leave. I felt that we had done enough today. There wasn't going to be a story about the new Center. There wasn't going to be a new Center. Not if the rabbi was going to stop all of the construction.

I was the confused one now. Why would he forgive or forget in such a way?

"Thank you, Rabbi. I think I should probably go now. It seems to be getting late and I have taken enough of your time."

"Yes. I know. You are confused, Chanele. Justice. Right? You want justice. But what is justice and where does it come from? From us? From you? From me? No. Justice comes from the Almighty. And only He can bring about true justice."

I nodded. As I stood up I looked at the desk. "Oh, your pills, Rabbi, don't forget to take your pills."

I got up and the Rabbi began to rise as well, knocking over some papers and a wooden box. "Oye, look at me. Old and clumsy."

"No, please don't get up. I can show myself out."

"Chanele," I turned around. "I mean Ms. Slone. Look what I found." He was holding the key.

"The key," I said, looking at its shiny surface and rather large shape.

"The Master Key," he said. Smiling now. As he looked at me, I felt he was looking into me. Figuring me out. Telling me something.

"Well, a shame not to need it," I said.

Has there ever been a time in your life when you felt that justice wasn't served?

_____

_____

_____

_____

_____

_____

_____

_____

_____

_____

_____

_____

_____

_____

_____

_____

V. Returning the Key

I was heading home, when I realized that I still had Rivka's keys and that her parents weren't far from here. So I stopped by. It was a chance to see Rivka again before she headed back to Israel. When I got to her parents house so many childhood memories came back to me. Hopscotch on the front walk, stoopball on the steps.

We ended up sitting on the stoop. She had just put Yosef to sleep and as she whispered, we headed outside. We talked and talked. She showed me a photo of her husband. "He is so handsome," I said. "Oh, sorry, can I say that about a rabbi?"

"Of course, you can," Rivka reassured me. "He is just like everybody else, you know." I felt relaxed around her, like I could say anything. Yet she had such a regal appearance and she spoke with such refinement. She was always confident and caring, but now, I heard more depth in her voice. Perhaps it was motherhood or marriage? Maybe it was religion or God?

"So," I said cautiously, "What is it like being so religious? Do you miss having fun?"

"What do you mean having fun?"

"You know, like going out and dancing or eating cheeseburgers? The things we used to do."

"Sometimes I think about how I used to be. Living without the mitzvos (or Jewish law). Living in Israel is amazing and exciting. Also, I feel complete and fulfilled spiritually."

"Spiritually? What do you mean?"

"Since I have taken on being an observant Jew, I feel close to something greater than what I see. Sometimes I feel like my heart is going to overflow with joy."
"Getting married is wonderful and romantic. Having a child is magical and deeply meaningful." But, connecting to God, - praying and knowing He is with me - that is my

personal time when I feel most spiritual, most complete. Fulfilled."

I looked in her eyes as she spoke and they were so clear. I looked up at the sky. There were stars everywhere.

"It is all so big. The universe. How do you know He is with you?"

"Faith is a part of it, but truth is the most significant part of faith. Believing that your life is all good and it is designed and meant to be unique and special. Only for you.

"Prayer is a way to keep us close to God. Like knowing a friend is there for us. Like when we talk and keep in touch, this keeps us close to the truth that we are not alone. God is truly with each of us. When we pray, we feel it more."

Rivka was so convincing.

Rivka has complete faith in the Almighty. I long to have such faith. How do you develop your faith?

I left Rivka feeling invigorated. I enjoyed our time together as always. Although she appeared so different she was the same person I had always known and loved. She made sense.

As I traveled home, on two subways and a bus, I was still fixated on the rabbi's words and couldn't get past his vociferous decision not to rebuild the Center. The core. That is what he called it. How could he, after all these years, just turn away? Turn his back on the community?

His words were so distant. I felt throughout our time together that he was distancing himself from me, from the reality of what had happened. He seemed so lost.

Lost? A rabbi? Is that possible? Yet he knew so much and felt so deeply for the Torah and for God. Why was he willing to give up? I said a silent prayer for him. That he should find the strength of will to persevere. That he should be healed physically and spiritually. I said a silent prayer for him...

> "Heal us, God, then we will be healed. Save us then we will be saved. For You are our praise. Bring complete recovery for all our ailments. For You are God, King, faithful and compassionate healer. Blessed are You, God, Who heals the sick of His people Israel."

Have you ever been sick and in need of healing? How did you push yourself to recuperate? Did you pray? Have you ever prayed for others who were suffering?

It was so late when I finally got home. I collapsed on the bed and didn't even get undressed. Brooklyn is far away! Not only did I feel like I had traveled physically far but the exhaustion I felt made me think it was more than that.

I had gone back. I had done it. Thinking about Brooklyn over all these years and feeling like I was so far removed from that life. Yet going back today and spending time there; I was feeling closer. Closer to what, though? Closer to my past? Closer to whom? My Bubby, sure. My great grandparents? Closer to my roots. My neighborhood. Sure. It is always fun to see old streets and doorways that once marked friendships and birthday parties. Mentally replaying hopscotch and stoopball, seeing people from the past. It is all meaningful. I could have left it at that. But there was more today. I felt more today. Closer to my heritage - to my family. I do feel closer to myself, closer than I have in a while.

Are you like Hannah, who has moved away from her familiar roots, neighborhood and relationships? If so, how has the distance affected you? Have you changed? If so, do you ever wish you could change the past?

_____
_____
_____
_____
_____
_____
_____
_____
_____
_____
_____
_____

Hannah's Second Dream

There is a terrible fire. People are shouting and screaming everywhere. "Run, Hannah, Run. Jerusalem is burning!" I heard a voice yell out through the smoke.

"Here I am, Father. I am running away. But where will I go?"

"Here, here, just reach your hand to me I am over here. Can you see me?"

"No, I can't see you, Father, please, come to me, come with me and show me where to go.

"Father! Father!"

"I can't. I must stay and put out the flames. Take the key, Chanele." I reached out and grabbed it.

"Run. Now run as fast and far as you can."

I am running. I feel my legs strain and stretch. The flames are too high, the fire is rising and the smoke is thick and black. I am running through the flames. I am sweating, it is an inferno around me and I won't get out. I won't be saved. I clutch the key so close to me. Closer, closer.

I have called out to God and He has saved me and heard my call. Have you called Him, lately? Why?

_____

_____

_____

_____

_____

_____

_____

_____

_____

_____

_____

Awakened

I woke in a pool of sweat. 5 a.m. I lay there, drenched and still fully dressed. My eyes were closed tightly. I was afraid to open them, yet desperate to leave the terrible place I had just been.

Where had I been? Why had I been there? A dream so real. A place I had known. But when? Where?

Hannah's dream is so vivid. Have you ever had a repetitive dream, one that stays with you well past morning?

_____
_____
_____
_____
_____
_____
_____
_____
_____
_____
_____
_____
_____
_____
_____
_____
_____
_____
_____
_____

I had to write this dream down. So I grabbed my journal.

So much running through my head. The fire was so real I felt that heat was penetrating my skin.
I showered and skipped my morning routine today.

I figured between visiting Brooklyn, talking to Rivka and the burning of Jerusalem, I was covered if I had missed a day of my personal prayers with my Bubby's siddur.

I showered. First hot, then cold.

How do morning rituals affect your mood throughout the day? Have you ever skipped a portion of your routine to save time and regretted it later?

TGIF! Thank God it's Friday. The weekend is here and I can put the paper and the rabbi aside for a few days and enjoy time with my family. Before I left the City, there were a few errands I needed to do. I also wanted to pick up a few things for the weekend. There was a bakery on West 75th that had the best bobka.

Maybe Miriam will even give birth this weekend! Now that she is in her ninth month. Full term. How exciting and beautiful it will be to see a newborn, my niece or nephew. My sister's first child. Ben is so excited, too. He is going to be a great father.

I started thinking about myself. "Soon by you," was the catch phrase that everyone always felt compelled to say when I entered any room where there were family members between the ages of 45 and 92. That is also what I will have to look forward to this weekend. I will have to put up with it. When I was younger, it didn't bother me. Nowadays it did; it bothered me. It never annoyed me when Bubby said it, though.

"Soon by you, Chanele," she would say. It almost sounded like a song. I don't remember the first time Bubby said those words to me. I must have been seven or eight. I remember blushing at the thought of me as a bride. We were sitting at a wedding at the Center. The very building I had visited yesterday, as a grown woman. The Center, the rabbi and the memories of the meeting came haunting back. But the memory of my childhood came rushing back, overpowering the most recent experience.

"Chanele," Bubby said as she called me over and gave me a rich, thick kiss on the cheek. "Look at the kallah, bride" she smiled. "She is so beautiful with her dress flowing and her veil. What a day, filled with hope and love. This is what I pray for you, my sweet sister." She always called me her sister.

I never met my Tanta Hannah. She perished in the Holocaust. For as long as I knew my Bubby, she was alone.

No sister, no husband. Just Bubby. She lived with us on Avenue J since before I was born.

Then, as she held on to my hand, she whispered, "Soon by you, Chanele. Soon by you." I laughed at the thought. Blushing, I shouted, "I am only seven, Bubby."

"Nu? Today you're seven and tomorrow will be here before you know it."

"Huh?" Bubby always said things I didn't quite get. But they were filled with her unconditional love and eternal wisdom. I knew that much.

I was right there with her when she passed away. We were standing in the kitchen and she was boiling a chicken. She was always boiling a chicken or eating borscht. It was so sudden. I was 16 years old. I remember it like it was yesterday.

So we were at the wedding, at the Center. The kallah was gorgeous and glowing. The chatan was stunning and sharply dressed. I was so in awe of the romance of it all. Yes, love is romantic. So they say. These days I am just looking for compatible.

"Soon by you," Bubby would say, so long ago. "Soon by me," I still silently hoped.

I completed my errands in a rushed, yet calm, state of mind. I wanted to help the rabbi see how important it was to rebuild the Center. I couldn't figure out why I cared so much. I rarely went home. I was a Manhattan girl now. No longer was I even remotely interested in being a shtetl-goer, small towner.

Returning to the mediocrity of Brooklyn, the familiarity of a place where everyone knows your business. No thank you. I loved the pace of the big city. I loved that I could be anonymous if I wanted to. I loved the bagels at the corner bakery, the drinks at my favorite pub on the West Side, and the new musicians every Thursday night in the Village.

The thought of spending an entire Friday night in Brooklyn was overwhelming. Shabbat dinner tonight, at my parents, was a bit of a chore. I loved them so much but I hadn't chosen the life they wanted for me. Even though I felt uncomfortable going back, they did love having me there. I took a deep breath and focused on the joy I would be bringing my parents tonight.

VI. Shabbos

As the train inched to a stop, I noticed the familiar smells of Brooklyn. Sounds gross, I know, but to a nostalgic nose it was quite aromatic. As I left the station and headed toward home I thought of the Center. I would be passing it in just a moment.

Should I stop over to say Shabbat shalom to the rabbi? It was such an awkward goodbye yesterday. He would probably be getting ready for shul and his wife, she would be preparing the house and setting the table. We would have a nice dinner filled with the traditional Shabbat foods. Dad still went to shul, more for the schmoozing than the praying. Ben always went. Shabbat was a time for us to get together, although a lot less often than it used to be.

As I walked, I saw the sign for the future home of the NEW Brooklyn Jewish Center. Only I knew it wasn't really going to happen. And Rabbi Marcus, that is. His home was just next door so I decided to go over and say Good Shabbos. As I approached the door it opened and out came the rabbi in full Shabbat garb. Black coat and black hat.

He looked taller and more impressive than before. "Hannah," he said, surprised. "Gut Shabbos."

"Good Shabbos, Rabbi. I was in the neighborhood and thought I would just come say hello. I am on my way to my parents for Shabbat."

"How nice Chanele. Come, walk with me a moment." "Sure," I said reluctantly, but at the same time I was eager to have more time with this humble yet strong man. His eyes were so kind and so tired. I couldn't stop looking into them. Just then his grandson approached, the one from yesterday. He also looked taller and a bit older than I had thought.

"Moshe, this is Chan...I mean, Hannah."

"How are you," I asked.

"Good Shabbos, Hello."

We walked a bit and then the rabbi mentioned the Center. "Hannah, I know my decision surprises you. You're upset, no?"

"I am sorry Rabbi. I just feel that you are giving up, I guess. I looked at his grandson walking a foot ahead. He was listening to us, I was sure.

"The Center serves more than just the older generation, today, Rabbi. I went there myself as a girl. Even the less religious enjoyed its safety and warmth. Now you are thinking of, what, closing up shop and that is it?"

"Someone else will come along and begin a new project. A new way of bringing people together. I don't have the ideas anymore," he went on. "And I am tired. Look at me. How much more can I do?"

"Tired. You don't know what tired is." I went on. "I haven't slept in days - I keep having these dreams. These ridiculous dreams about a key and fire and... and I don't know what else." I couldn't believe I just blurted that out.

"Go on," said the rabbi, "What about this key?"

"I don't know, I am supposed to find this key, or reach out for it, and it will open something. Unlock something..."

"Something eternal," he said.

"Yes," I hesitated.

I glanced at my watch. We were standing outside the shul, a small structure, old, and what he referred to as a shteible. We were at the corner of Avenue J and Ocean Parkway. "Well, it is getting late, Good Shabbos, Rabbi."

"I will see you at the opening of the Center, right? Rabbi, I *will* see you?"

"Good Shabbos, Hannah," he nodded. I continued walking a few more blocks, thinking about why it has taken so long for me to return to these streets of my childhood. I knew part of it was that I felt guilty that I wasn't considered as religious anymore. Not eating kosher, not keeping Shabbos, the way I had as a girl.

But the street wasn't as scary and distant as I thought it would be. In fact, as I watched the children lighting candles with their mothers and the boys walking to shul with their fathers. I couldn't help feeling that I was still a part of this world somehow.

Could it be that the very thing that had been keeping me away for so long was the one thing that was actually bringing me back?

Returning home was scary for Hannah, but at the same time she felt closer to something. How do you feel when you return to your family or childhood home?

I walked up the front path and entered the house. The lights were dimly lit. The candles were set by the window.

"Mom, I'm home!" I shouted. The sound level was a complete contrast to the quiet peace that was warming the home. I slowly entered the kitchen, the heart of the home. Mom and Miriam were there sampling the soup.

"Yum!" I said. Smiling ear to ear as they looked up equally thrilled at the sight of me.

"Can I have a taste?" I walked over as mom placed an oversized spoon in the steaming bowl upon the stove. Before it entered my mouth I closed my eyes, smelled the broth and hoped that the tip of my tongue would feel the sting of the liquid, that way I could relive this memory for a few more days.

"Where's Dad?" I asked, simply enough. "At shul, for a change, with Ben" added Miriam. "Oh," I responded. "Let me help set the table, Mom."

"Sure."

The dining room was a combination of a dark wood table and chairs with rustic hutches filled with chachkies and chachkies (knicknacks) from our childhood, Shabbos candle holders, menorahs and challah covers. They had also collected the most elegant array of Israeli-style art and recently purchased a hand-carved wine rack. I walked over and chose a sweet Bartenuro. I placed it on the table beside dad's Kiddush cup.

"Hey, Mom, where is my kiddush cup?" I looked in the hutch. "It should be there," she called out. "Take a look behind the new Lenox figure we bought."

As I dug it out of the back shelf, behind a, who knows what, ornate statue of a girl holding what appeared to be a... key? I held it tightly and took it out of its home. I looked at the bottom of the small figure. Eternal Key. I felt a ball clog my throat. Swallow, I told myself. Why was she obsessed with these little delicate figurines? They are so ridiculous. I put it back clumsily and with aggravation.

I stared at my cup and noticed the dent along the rim. A tooth mark I put there as a two-year-old. I let my finger rub along the rim and felt that emptiness again.

The call from dad, "Kiddush girls," echoed in my ears. He always called us in the plural form, "girls," including Mom.

Even years ago, when I was still in high school and Miriam went off to seminary in Jerusalem.

Kiddush was a special time. The dimly lit room, the smells of Shabbos, the challah and dad's kiddush.

As if our family had been making this blessing for centuries.

As if dad was connecting us with our past each and every Friday night. Did Kiddush do that? Did a blessing have the power to do that? Did it have the power to connect us all to our past and help us find our future?

The cup was always filled to the top, overflowing and dripping on the plate beneath.

"Blessed are You, God, King of the Universe who commands us on the blessing of Kiddush."

He always ended with the same additional blessing. "May our lives be filled to the top with the sweetness of the Shabbos."

Once I asked him why, and he said, "That is the way our family has always done it."

How we had always done it? Since when? How far back, I wondered?

Do you have a day of the week, month, or year that stands out from the rest? If so, why? How do you observe that special date?

"Good Shabbos girls," Dad yelled happily. We had such a perfect time. Laughing and lounging around the table. I truly didn't want it to end.

Dinner was delicious and I was stuffed and, not to mention, exhausted. To the point where I decided to stay over at my parents' home. I hadn't done that in years.

Over the past five years there was always a place to be on a Friday night. Friends were meeting up at West 72nd or there was a great jazz band playing in the Village. "So, Hannah, nothing to run home to tonight?" Dad felt he had a right to ask. Before I could answer he was grabbing sheets and blankets from the front hall closet. I guess he was excited to have me home.

Since I had decided to stay I could linger at the table eating the desserts and enjoying some more wine. Miriam was trying her best to stay seated although I could tell the baby must have been moving and shaking, because she couldn't sit still.

"Miriam," said Ben, motioning toward her, "Come, I'll move you to the couch."

"I'll come too," I said, taking my wine and bobka cake along. We sat together and didn't stop laughing about the past, about our girlhood antics, like sharing clothes. Miriam hated sharing clothes with me. "You were always such a mess," she said. "As soon as you would put it on it didn't matter what it was, it got dirty. A spilled drink, a dropped cookie, you name it."

We both laughed as we noticed the wine stain on my shirt and the chocolate spot on my pants.

"It's late," said Ben. "We better get home. The walk will do us good," he said, as he grabbed the underbelly of his... belly. "The walk will do *you* good," she said. "You have more baby weight to lose than I do," Miriam refuted.

I helped her up and kissed her goodnight. "Call us if anything happens." "Not on Shabbos," added Dad!

Mom rushed in, "Of course on Shabbos, I'll pick up," she whispered. "I must know immediately! You know that." We knew that, alright.

"Call with your elbow or dial with a spoon," she said. As if she had her own Laws of Shabbos.

"We know, Mom, you have the book called, "Shabbos as it applies to soon-to-be Bubbies.""

This Shabbos was better than I could have imagined. In fact, it almost made me forget about my time with the rabbi and my dreams. I was glad no one mentioned the bags under my eyes. I didn't want to recount the awful nights I had been having.

"Miriam looks so great, Mom, doesn't she? She is so ready to give birth," I added. Mom looked at me with a gleam of excitement in her eyes as well as a bit of fear.

"I know you worry about her, but she is healthy and she and the baby will be fine. Healthy and fine," I said confidently.

"Now, let's get you settled." We cleared the table and I caught another glimpse of that Lenox figure. "Mom, when did you get that?"

"What?" she asked.

I held up the Eternal Key figure. "This."

"Oh, I just found it a few days ago. Funny, I hadn't bought a new Lenox in years and I was shopping downtown and saw this in the window. I literally walked right in and bought it. Just like that. Isn't it sweet and sad at the same time?"

"What do you mean?" I asked.

"Well, she looks a bit lost. Like she is searching. I felt like I needed her and like she needed me. I know, you can laugh at me all you want," she said.

"Mom, you're so sappy and so deep at the same time. But, I love you the way you are."

"I am who I am," she said. "Love you, sweetie." She closed the door behind her.

I got comfortable in an old pair of sweats and a T-shirt. I was starting to dose, when I suddenly remembered to say the bedtime prayer. I hadn't done it in so long but, in this room, my childhood bed, on this night I felt so nostalgic, so safe, so young. I began to say the bedtime Shema. By heart.

The Bedtime Shema
"Hear, oh Israel, the Lord our God, the Lord is One."

I fell into a deep sleep. Too deep of a sleep to dream, I hoped. Instead of thinking about the dream and the Center, I thought about how thankful I felt to have such strong women in my life. Mom and Miriam are both such wonderful examples of beautiful and confident women.

Do you have a female role model, like a mother, who molded you into the person you are today?

_____

_____

_____

_____

_____

_____

_____

_____

_____

_____

_____

_____

_____

_____

Awakened II

Suddenly Hannah's eyes opened wide. She could feel something was happening and as soon as she sat up her mother appeared at the doorway.

"She's in labor. Miriam is having the baby! Come, we must go with her to the hospital." I dressed quickly and we ran down to the street. It was dark with a few dimly lit street lamps showing us the way.

Ben called the cab and with an envelope, filled with exact change, and at the ready, we all piled in. Miriam in back with mom and Ben and I in the front.

I stared at her, my head turned 180 degrees, the whole time. She's beautiful. Miriam's amazing. Strong and calm. Breathing and closing her eyes. Mom rubs her back and holds her hand. I truly did not think I would be a part of her birth experience.

I thought I would be the aunt who came over the next day with a onesie and teddy bear. But I am going to be with her. With Miriam, delivering her baby. I am so excited. I don't feel tired, although it is about 1 a.m. I am totally focused on Miriam.

We arrived at the hospital at 1:35 a.m. Miriam looked a bit more stressed now. Ben got her a wheel chair and then the nurse wheeled her to the birth pavilion.

Birth Pavilion? Miriam had told me about it months ago but now seeing it, I actually felt like it was a beautiful, calming space. It made me feel so happy for her and her future. A wave of relief and joy spread over me. We registered her and they settled her in. When Dr. Jacob arrived he told us we would have a long night ahead of us so, "sit tight," he said.

Mom and I got a cup of coffee and waited. Then, Ben came out and brought us into the room. Miriam was propped up in bed and breathing steadily. She was so strong, I kept saying to myself. Of course she is strong, she is my big sister.

For as long as I can remember, Miriam paved the way for me and my opportunities. She was always there for me to talk to. When she left for seminary and then for college we started to drift apart. When I decided not to go to seminary, she told me how disappointed she was and that I was making a mistake.

From then on she seemed distant, even when she met Ben, she waited awhile before introducing us. She was upset with me for my religious choices. I ignored her and felt abandoned.

Luckily, we have been getting close again. Lately, I felt that she was opening up to me even though we were different in many ways. We were sisters and that was always going to bind us together.

Not only were we sisters but I was going to help her and be there for her as she gave birth to her first child.

I was holding Miriam's hand the whole time she was in labor. She began to push and I was right there with her. A thought kept coming back to me over and over. A blessing mom had always said as she lit the candles...

"May we be blessed in the spirit of Sara, Rivka, Rachel and Leah, our mothers, and may your countenance shine so that you are saved."

Miriam had a boy that night. It was the most spectacular night of my life.

Have you ever been part of something so incredible with someone else that you felt your life was changed forever? How did the experience affect you and why did it affect you in such a way?

_____

_____

_____

_____

_____

_____

_____

_____

_____

_____

_____

_____

_____

_____

_____

_____

_____

_____

_____

_____

_____

_____

_____

_____

_____

_____

_____

_____

_____

_____

VII. The Upper West Side

I returned home in the early morning hours and found my cell phone on the counter where I had accidentally left it a day and half ago. First, "Where is the story, Hannah? We go to print in two days! The press is all over this story and who is this rabbi who's being difficult?"

The next message was from Moshe, the Rabbi's grandson. "My grandfather took a terrible turn and is in the hospital. He is at Brooklyn Community. Please come as soon as you can." I quickly grabbed my purse and ran out the door.

The paper? The hospital? Where was I heading? I didn't even know myself when I left the apartment. What could he possibly have to tell me? I felt that knot in my throat and that queasy feeling in my stomach.

Fifty minutes later I ended up in front of the hospital. I hesitatingly walked into the emergency room entrance. I saw Moshe. He was pacing the hall mumbling to himself. "Moshe? Moshe?" He turned and I saw he was still mumbling. I realized he was praying. I didn't realize you could pray anywhere you were. Or any time of day.

"What happened?" I asked.

"Hannah. It's my grandfather. After Shabbos, he started having difficulty breathing and he looked pale so we brought him to the hospital."

"They are telling us that he had a stroke. He isn't making sense right now but he insisted that I call you and bring you to him immediately. Thank you so much for coming."

"Of course. I feel terrible about Rabbi Marcus. I'm so sorry." I didn't mention the other message on my machine. It's my problem not theirs.

"Please, can I bring you into the room? He keeps asking for you." "Sure, but will they let me in? I am not family," I commented. "We will say you're my sis....wife."

We walked. The word "wife" lingered in my head.

VIII. Family Ties

The corridor seemed never-ending. We took the elevator to intensive care. We barely spoke. He was so serious and sad. I looked at this young man's eyes. They were older than his years. They were blue. They were deeply worn, as if they had seen so many things, so many places, yet they seemed to find beauty and light even in the darkest spaces.

"He wants to talk with you. He keeps mentioning this key. A master key?"

"Yes. He was looking for it the other day. He was frantically looking for the master key. The one that was needed to open the lockbox of documents needed for the Center. He mentioned it to me."

"What about the fire? He keeps saying that you will know how to put out the fire?"

I was sure he must be talking about the fire in the Center. The one I am interviewing him about.

Now, I was conjuring up the memory of our previous meeting and his ramblings about the fire and not finding the key. I didn't say anything. I was cautious about sharing too much information about his rantings and my dreams.

He opened the door and escorted me into the Rabbi Marcus' hospital room. He lay there on the bed. Tubes all over him. He looked so old now; frail. Not like the man with the fire in his eyes that had spoken with me just days earlier.

I slowly approached the bed.

"A boy," said the rabbi. Mazal tov on the baby boy, Hannah."

"Thank you. Rabbi. But how did you know?"

The rabbi just smiled at me as I took a seat. I observed his tranquil presence. His genuine calm amidst such pain.

He closed his eyes. "Shhhhh," said his grandson.

"Why?" I wondered out loud. "Is he sleeping?"

"No," said Moshe. "He is praying." I stood silent.

I closed my eyes and tried to feel what he must feel, when he prays. It also just felt like the right thing to do. His eyes were closed so tightly, I could see them quiver. I was silent and waited for him to speak again.

Why had I come here? I wondered.

"Hannah, your dreams?" he said. He knew a bit about them, from the other night. But I hadn't shared the intimate details? "Yes, Rabbi?" I questioned. "Have you had any others? Any new dreams - about the fires or the Temple?" I was afraid to recount the dream I had the other night. It was so violent and real. It would be embarrassing to share it. Especially with Moshe standing in the room.

"Fire, yes. A fire, and I was running from it. Others were standing around and I was running without looking back. No one was putting it out but there was a voice calling to me, saying, 'Run, run Hannah, and take the key.' He reached out to hand me something. I was screaming to Him, Father, Father please come with me, but he wouldn't. I woke up in a pool of sweat, burning up."

I could tell that the rabbi was getting a bit aggravated. He was beginning to tense up. Moshe approached and spoke to his grandfather in Yiddish, I think. Then, the rabbi seemed out of breath. I felt it was time to go. I motioned a wave and walked toward the door.

"I am so sorry, I didn't mean to excite him," I said.

"Of course. I know he wanted to hear more about your dream. He cares for you, Hannah."

"So, now what?" I asked.

"We will have to wait. See how his tests come back." With a stroke, they never know how much damage there was. My grandmother is tired, I am going to bring her home and then I will come back later, with a minyan."

"You care for him so much. You are so good to him, I can see."

"He is my grandfather. The keeper of all that I know. He taught me everything. Torah, chesed, kindness. He even taught me how to make potato latkes. He makes the best latkes. Every Chanukah I would come for the week. We would go to the Shoprite and buy bags and bags of potatoes and onions, and so much oil."

He smiled, took a deep breath and tears filled his deep eyes. I looked away. I didn't want to intrude on his pain.

Just then, Leah Marcus appeared. She was so elegant and regal looking. She wore a long robe and a scarf perfectly tied around her head.

"He is resting calmly now," Leah commented. "I kissed him and told him I would be back this evening. There is much to be done at home if the Center will reopen as scheduled. Even though he is fighting it, he knows it must be done. I will not let his dreams disappear. All he has worked for. All he has done. He is not thinking straight. He is exhausted. But we must continue to build."

"I heard my grandfather wished you a mazal tov. Who had a baby," asked Moshe?

"Oh, my sister had a boy last night. I was actually just here, a few hours ago. How did the rabbi know? Moshe looked away and shrugged his shoulders. "I don't know?"

"In fact, as soon as I walked into my apartment early this morning from the birth, I heard your message and turned around and came back."

"Well, mazal tov to your family," said Mrs. Marcus. "And soon by you, Hannah. You know we have known your parents for such a long time. And you since you were a little girl."

Have you ever been involved with something that was bigger than just you?

I smiled but felt a bit embarrassed that I hadn't come home too much lately.

"Thank you for coming all the way back. You did a mitzvah. By the way, my husband is a fan of your writing, you know," added Mrs. Marcus.

As I turned to leave, I heard Moshe say, "Soon by you, Hannah, you will make someone a wonderful wife one day." I wanted to turn around and smile at him, but I was blushing too much.

55 minutes later... home sweet home. What should I do first? My editor did not want to let this story go. Of course not, I was the one to convince him that it was a major change that was happening in the city and that by getting the exclusive on this, he would not only be shaking the mayors' hand at the official groundbreaking but we would even get the credit for getting a convicted criminal off the streets.

I had spent too much time on it, too much time explaining that with a little more time, not only will we have a story about a new Jewish Center, but I bet I would be able to convince the rabbi to persecute the arsonist.

I was certain it was a guy from the neighborhood. I knew the rabbi would want justice. Now that I met his grandson, I was sure they would both want justice. A few more days were all I needed.

But as of yesterday, I have a new nephew which means that my sister needs me. Rabbi Marcus, my primary source, is in the hospital, a criminal has not been brought to true justice, and I haven't slept in days because of these haunting dreams.

I arrived at the paper and was immediately signaled into the editor's office.

"Hi Joe."

"Hello Hannah. My disappearing ghost writer," he chuckled.

"Funny. Listen, before you say anything, can you at least say congratulations?"

"Why?"

"Well, my sister had a baby last night."

"Oh, congratulations and mazal tov. Now, can we get down to deadlines? I needed your story on the Center yesterday and I don't know the time we set for the press conference? Have you called the mayor's office?

"The press conference, huh," mumbled Hannah?

"Yes, the press conference where the mayor and the police chief and this rabbi of yours are supposed to acknowledge that the criminal was caught and is behind bars, where he belongs. The press conference held at the construction site. Just eight days from now. Remember? People want justice. You're delivering that to them so that they can sleep at night.

"Don't get me wrong, the initial coverage you did last month on the fire and the arson suspects was amazing. And then, the rabbi's refusal to press charges, great stuff, really. Even Mayor Richmond coming up with city funds to rebuild the Center, terrific! But now, where are we? Where are you? Where are you? Hello?!"

"Oh, sorry, really I am listening. OK, so you want me to go back to Brooklyn, right? To finish the story. Eight days till the opening and press conference. Eight days, that is all I need. It is going to be great, I promise!" she shouted as she rushed back out to the busy street.

Eight days is going to be great. It will be my nephew's bris. Now, I have to get this story done. Finished. I promised! Eight days, like the eight days of Chanukah. Good, I need a miracle, too!

Have you ever made a promise that you were unable to keep? Did you ever wish you could take it back?

_____
_____
_____
_____
_____
_____
_____
_____
_____
_____
_____
_____
_____
_____
_____
_____
_____
_____
_____
_____
_____
_____
_____
_____
_____
_____
_____
_____
_____
_____
_____
_____

I picked up the phone even before I put my bag down. "Mom, can I stay with you guys for the rest of the week?"

"Sure," she responded. "Miriam will be so happy to have you nearby."

"I'm just going to pack a few things and be on my way. Love you. Bye."

Hanging up, I realized mom knew nothing about the details of the story. She and Dad, like most, thought Rabbi Marcus was being irrational and were terribly upset about his actions. I decided not to share too much with my parents.

In my mind I was certain that I could figure out a way to convince the rabbi to rebuild the Center.

Returning to Brooklyn, again, twice in one day - that was a bit much for me.

IX. A Deception at the Reception

Hannah arrived at the hospital after visiting hours but thanks to the earlier introduction as "Mrs. Hannah Marcus," she was easily able to enter to the rabbi's room, through the reception and nurses station.

The rabbi was wide awake and looked as if he was expecting her. Moshe was sitting beside him.

"Hannah. Good to see you," said Moshe. He sounded genuine.

"How is your nephew?"

"Adorable, thanks, I just peaked in on him in the nursery.

"And your sister, Miriam?"

"She is doing fine. Tired and excited at the same time."

"Baruch Hashem," he added. As he said those words, with God's blessing, I instantly felt comfortable.

Moshe was so easy to talk to. He was always attentive and I knew he truly cared about listening to what I had to say.

I have been on so many dates where the guy was completely disinterested in anything and everything I was saying. It has gotten to the point where I would make things up about my life, which by the way is already really interesting on its own, just to have some conversation during an already awkward dinner or, if I was lucky, just a coffee.

Trying desperately to get those thoughts out of my mind, I focused on the kindness of Moshe and his stature, so upright and confident. Yet, he was also completely warm and approachable.

The rabbi spoke up now. "So, Hannah, you've come back."

"Well, you asked for me, Rabbi, and I don't feel we finished our conversation. I want you to tell me more.

"What more is there to tell?" asked Rabbi Marcus.

"Please," I insisted, "tell me about the Center, the night of the fire."

"But, that is just a part of it. There is still more, than that, right, Hannah? There is more than just writing a story and getting the attention for getting the story. Right, Chanele?" asked Rabbi Marcus.

"What do you mean?"

"Hannah, how long has it been since you spent this much time in your neighborhood? How long has it been since you slept over on Shabbos at your parents' home on Avenue J?"

"I don't know, maybe six years?" As I said it I couldn't believe my own words. Six years was a long time to abandon my home, my neighborhood, everything I knew. But, I have been busy making a life for myself, I justified in my head.

"It is not as though I don't care about my home, my family and my community, Rabbi. It is just that I moved on."

"Yes, moving on is important at the right time, but not when you are needed," said Rabbi Marcus.

"Exactly. And now look at what you are doing. Moving on, Rabbi, you are leaving the community that still needs you so much. How can you say you care, when you are abandoning everyone?"

I couldn't believe what I had just blurted out. "I am so sorry, Rabbi."

"No. It's OK, Hannah. We were brought together for a reason, you know."

I knew that I felt some connection to the rabbi, but I didn't want to admit it.

"We both truly care about the community and the Center and it is time for all of us to return home."

"Who do you mean?" I asked.

"You, me. Moshe. We all move on, Hannah, yes, but it doesn't mean we have to move away."

I sat down. What did he expect of me? My heart rate was pulsing and I was feeling sick to my stomach, again. "Hannah, look at me. Caring about something is good, Hannah. Caring so much about something that you will stop at nothing to find it, that is good, too - for the right reasons."

"Like finding the truth, right?" I asked.

"But maybe the truth, all along, is not about the fire in the Center. It is finding out what is burning inside of you," Rabbi Marcus urged.

I sat frozen. I was thinking and thinking about what to say next. Should I allow myself the luxury of having a breakdown right now, allowing the tears that had been welling up for months to flow?

The clarity that was coming to me more easily now than ever before was frightening. Because with clarity like this I could no longer deny what I must do.

With clarity comes change. Is there anything you have been hiding from, any truth or change that you want to make in your life? How would you approach it?

X.   Back to Business

"Rabbi, may I please ask you why you didn't press charges? You saw the man, didn't you? You were in the Center when it happened, in your study. You could have brought justice to all the people. You could have brought peace to the community. Why didn't you choose to speak up against him?"

"Oy, Hannah. For so long I have been watching the neighborhood. The children learning, the families growing. Alongside so much pain and turmoil."

"What do you mean? Pain?"

"Our small, little shteible, our Center of Torah and mitzvos hasn't been alone on an island. We have been a part of a larger world. We are a part of the anger that rages and part of the conflict and confusion among others. The whites, the blacks, the Jews, the non-Jews; it's all the same.

"That doesn't answer my question. Why didn't you help put away the arsonist? It would have been the right and just thing to do."

"Why? Was he the only one to blame?"

Coughing and struggling for breath, the rabbi grabbed his water. "Let me get it for you, Rabbi." I handed him the water.

Hesitatingly, I asked, "What did you mean earlier, when you said I was chasing a story?"

"You're running fast. All the time. Writing in your little book. About this one and that one. You are chasing something, searching for what? For whom?"

"I just want to get to the truth. About the person or the story. Why is that wrong?"

"It isn't wrong. It's fine. If that is what you want. But, know that you are always going to be searching for another story or chasing after another version of the truth. Until..."

"Until what?"

"Until you look inside yourself and stop running. Rest, sleep, sometimes even in our dreams we find the key to what we are looking for. The searching doesn't have to be going on around you. It should be stirring inside you."

It was getting late and I could see Rabbi Marcus was getting tired.

"I think I should go and check on Miriam and the baby, now. Thank you for your time, Rabbi."

"I'm going to rest now. Please come back tomorrow. I want to tell you more about the Center and the future of the neighborhood. It will all work out. It is all God's will."

XI. The Void of Fear

I went over to the maternity ward hoping to see Miriam and the baby snuggled together getting to know one another. I wanted to spend a moment with them enjoying such a blessing. I knocked on the door.

Again. Strange. A sudden pang of nerves raced through me and I shivered.

I turned and, just as I did, I saw my parents and Ben walking down the hall. "Mom, Dad?" I ran over. "What's the matter? Where's Miriam and the baby?" Their faces were pale and their eyes looked empty. As if they were stunned and speechless.

"Miriam and the baby have high fevers. They are not sure why, but they were moved to ICU. It just happened." I grabbed my mother's hand it was cold as ice and I could see she was frozen with fear.

"What do we do?"

"We wait. Let's go to the lobby and soon the doctor will come and tell us what is happening."

We sat and waited. And waited. Almost an hour later and lifetime away the doctor came out and told us that the two of them had been put on antibiotics and were resting comfortably.

It could be a virus. It sometimes happens, he said, their resistance is low and there is something that happens called group B strep that can be serious if it is not caught on time.

"Was this on time?" I asked.

"It should have been caught before delivery." That was all he said. Then he walked away down the long cold hallway and through these huge double doors that said Emergency Staff Only.

I was tired. I was angry with the rabbi. I was scared for Miriam and the baby. I was feeling empty.

Have you ever felt so empty and scared that you didn't know if you would ever "fill up" again?

I fell asleep and woke to Moshe at my side. When I looked up, I saw him. He had his eyes closed tightly shut and was mumbling under his breath. Praying. For Rabbi Marcus. For Miriam. For the baby.

When he opened his eyes he looked at me. "Hannah, my grandfather told me what happened to your sister and nephew. I know they will be fine."

"Is it morning? Have I slept here all night?"

"It looks that way. Here, I brought you some coffee."

"Oh, thanks. How is the rabbi feeling?"

"He is sleeping, his sleep is so disturbed these days."

"I know how he feels," I said.

Just then I saw my parents and Ben. "So?"

"The fever broke. Thank God. They are doing well and resting, and she is nursing right now. You can come see. The baby has color and so does Miriam."

"You knew, Moshe? How?"

"None of us knows. It is that we pray. I have faith in God."

I believe in God, too, Hannah thought, but didn't dare say what she was thinking.

"Belief is not necessarily faith, you know."

"What?" asked Hannah.

"I'm just saying that belief in God is great and important. But faith, emunah and bitachon in God is different. Really knowing He is here for you and will do what is best, that is what we strive for."

"Go, Hannah, go enjoy your sister and nephew. Wish them a refuah shelama (full recovery) from me and my family. I hope we will talk again, soon."

I turned away and felt a sudden comfort in Moshe's words and a certain confidence in him. I also thought about the words of the rabbi last night. Look inside myself. Search for my own story.

I rushed down the hall, breathing quickly, excited to see a healthy Miriam and a healthy baby. I spent an hour with Miriam and held the sweet innocent little boy. He was just like an angel. I felt a well of joy surging through my body.

Possibly, that good old biological clock that everyone talks about. I don't care what it is. I felt the joy and basked in the beauty of the moment. Live my story. This is part of my story. Part of my family's story. I was so hyper now with the relief of the baby's well-being and my sister's health. I wanted to shout out to the world how blessed I am feeling.

How do I celebrate this miracle? How am I able to show my extreme gratitude? Who do I tell?

I walked along the corridor and ended up at Rabbi Marcus' room. The nurse immediately recognized me as Mrs. Hannah Marcus, a member of his family.

She ran to me and, looking nervous, asked if I could step into the room.

"Yes," I said, quickly. "What is it?"

"It is the rabbi. He is slipping into a coma. His mumblings during sleep are signs of distress and we cannot seem to calm him down."

Mrs. Marcus was called and she is on her way down.

"Of course, your husband knows what is going on. He will be right back."

I was speechless. All of a sudden I panicked. I am not a member of this family, I wanted to say. But I felt that I was already in too deep and I didn't want to get anyone in trouble.

"Please, hurry," she said, "He is asking for you."

I slowly entered the rabbi's hospital room. I felt like such a fraud, such a terrible person. The lies. I am not supposed to be here.

"You are supposed to be here, Hannah," he mumbled, sounding weak and scared, as he answered her thoughts.

I looked at him. I tried to look into his eyes. I could see his pain. I could see his whole being. It was too much. I didn't want to be here. I didn't want to be a part of this. I felt that I was intruding on his personal space.

"We cannot choose what we want to become a part of, Hannah. It is God's plan for us. You, my child, are meant to be here. Your searching, your questions, your fears, all lead you right here.

"But why?" I asked, moving closer. I wanted to touch his hand to show my compassion and love for him. But I knew it was not allowed. It was a Jewish law that men and women do not touch unless they are husband and wife. I inched myself closer.

"I have seen so much," he continued. "I have had such a wonderful life. Giving to the Jewish people. Teaching and guiding Jewish souls, young and old. I didn't push the police to arrest the boy, I know. That is what brought you to me. It brought you back to the community. That was the big story you were chasing. You are searching for the answers to the fire. The burning."

"Yes. But why?"

"To teach you a lesson, maybe. To teach you that even though the justice you were looking for may not have been found, so much more has been.

"You can search and search and not find answers. You can demand justice, as you see it and it may never come. But in the end, you, Hannah, you have to be certain. Certain that all of your searching will lead you to the answers that are right for you, and you alone.

Just then, Moshe and Mrs. Marcus appeared at the doorway. I turned away from the rabbi for just a moment and...

An alarming sound occurred and then a rush of people in scrubs ran into the rabbi's room. They ushered us to the waiting room and closed the door.

Take a deep breath and think of a specific concern or difficult feeling you have and allow yourself the space to pray for comfort.

_____

_____

_____

_____

_____

_____

_____

_____

_____

_____

_____

_____

_____

_____

_____

_____

_____

_____

_____

_____

It was as if his words were flying all around me... the answers must be right for me and me, alone.

The rush of joy I had just experienced for Miriam and the baby had deflated and now I was filled with an emptiness and a ball of anguish in the pit of my stomach. I waited with Mrs. Marcus, Moshe and other members of the community. So many men were huddled together praying for this sweet and humble man. A man who had given so much of himself to others.

We stood in the waiting room for what seemed like hours of silent prayer. I closed my eyes and thought about the rabbi and tried to connect my thoughts to God. I wanted to pray for this man that brought me home. He brought me back to a place I had left. I felt things were changing for me.

We re-entered the room and as I peeked at Moshe, I saw his eyes were fluttering quickly and his mouth was moving, yet nothing was coming out. Part of him seemed far away. Moshe seemed at peace and not as scared as I was.

After a while he turned to me and asked me if I would say a few prayers for his grandfather.

"Me? I don't know how to really pray. What do I say?"

"Prayers are only reciting what is in your heart," he said. "Just try to focus on your feelings and let your heart and mind do the rest."

I thought for a moment about the encounters I'd had with Rabbi Marcus over the past week. Although it seemed like a short period of time, he seemed to know me. It felt as though the Rabbi knew me better than I knew myself. I wanted more time with him. I felt words welling up in my throat. I needed to spend more time with the Rabbi, Please God, heal him. Give me more time with him.

"Hannah, I hope this doesn't sound awful, but can you tell me anything about what my grandfather said to you?"

"He is very anxious about the Center. He doesn't want it to open."

"Did he say why?"

"No. Just that there is too much pain and confusion around. He said that he is scared for Jewish people to gather."

Days passed without a word. The rabbi just lay there in his hospital bed. The silence seemed permanent.

I sat there and prayed, in the way Moshe had taught me to do. It was a tranquil space and one that I felt peaceful in. I felt alone yet embraced by a history, a people and a faith that I had not felt before.

I began each prayer with a greeting. As if I was introducing myself each day to God. Surely he knew who I was by now. But it felt more personal, like I was having a real conversation with Him. I would pray for the rabbi's well-being and then I would add Miriam and her baby, the bris was just two days away now.

The baby was nursing well and Miriam was gaining her strength back more each day.

I think back to that beautiful day when she delivered and the fear and despair we all felt when she and the baby were in distress. The day she and the baby were getting well was the same day the Rabbi began slipping away.

Why, I kept thinking, had these two worlds collided so? Joy and suffering; the fire in my dreams with the fire of the Center; life with death?

The coma. Will Rabbi Marcus wake up? Will he tell me the answers? Has he already told me all the answers I needed to know?

I was about to leave the rabbi's room when suddenly his eyes opened and he looked at me.

"Chanele" he whispered. I ran to his side. "Your dream. The fire and the key."

"Yes?" I responded ready for the answer, the truth. "Under the desk in my study. You will find the justice you want there. Do what you know is right. Do it because you know the truth. Don't look back. Hold out your hand for it and all the answers will be yours. Take the key and go, run as fast as you can toward the truth."

The exact words from my dream were confronting me here, now.

"How will I know if it is the truth? But wait... Rabbi Marcus.... please, what about the key?"

Then, just like that, he was gone. The rabbi was gone. His eyes closed and his heart stopped. I felt cold and alone. I turned around and saw Moshe. He was standing in the doorway.

His face was tear-stained, his smile was gone.

But, as always, his eyes were filled with light.

I was frozen and could not move. I slowly rose to my feet and walked into the waiting room. Moshe and I sat there quietly.

I saw Mrs. Marcus. She was accompanied by her daughter and her sister. She was frail and sad, yet she was clearheaded and calm. The rabbi's body was moved to a place where he would be cared for and prepared for burial, immediately.

He was to be buried in Jerusalem. The body would be sent there, accompanied by Moshe, the next day. The funeral would be the same day as the bris of my new nephew. The day of the groundbreaking ceremony.

My emotions were everywhere. My feelings were dark and light. I felt that the time I had spent with Rabbi Marcus included some of the most meaningful moments of my life.

Yet, he also left me with so many questions and confusions. Not to mention the eerie things he said to me about the key. And my dreams. So much to take in. So much to process. So much to do.

My parents were expecting me to stay with them in Brooklyn for the next few days to help prepare for the bris. Yet something was telling me I should go to the Rabbi's funeral.

How could I think of not being at the bris of my nephew? Go to Israel? Was I crazy? Maybe they would not want me to go. I mean, it was one thing to pretend I was a member of the family at the hospital. But to go to Israel with them? Have I lost my mind?

No. I reconciled, of course, I will be at the bris of my nephew. It is the right thing to do. My family is counting on me. But on the other hand, there is Moshe and I feel so connected to him. I don't know why but it is so real to me. Will I jeopardize a future we may have by making the wrong decision?

Have you ever been torn between your needs and the needs of others? How did you reconcile that situation?

"Hannah," I heard Moshe's voice at a distance. He was there to take care of what needed to be done. I wanted to be more like him. I wanted to continue learning from him.

"Moshe," my eyes were facing downward. I was afraid to see his eyes filled with tears and pain. The light that always shone through them was hidden by his sadness.

"I must leave tonight," he went on. The EL AL flight was full and he had to make all of the arrangements for the body to be boarded, immediately.

I waited for Moshe to ask me to join him. But he didn't. Infact, he actually said something so amazing.

"Hannah, I wish I could be at the bris of your nephew alongside you, but I must bring my grandfather's body to Eretz Yisroel. It is always a better choice to be welcoming new life into the world, rather than saying goodbye."

"Of course," I said. "I understand." Did I understand?

"My grandfather was a tzaddik, a righteous man. His soul remains with us forever. It is his garment that I am burying. His body is simply a covering for the true man he was. His soul is the everlasting light that remains in the world."

Have you ever felt like you needed to be in two places at once?
How did you find your direction?

_____
_____
_____
_____
_____
_____
_____
_____
_____
_____
_____
_____
_____
_____
_____
_____
_____
_____
_____
_____
_____
_____
_____
_____
_____
_____
_____
_____

Moshe continued, "It is my job, my avodah, to see that his body is buried properly, according to Jewish law. Then I will return home and continue his work. But that is for another time."

Moshe paused, not ready to say goodbye.

"Hannah, I have been wanting to talk with you for a while now. It has all happened so quickly. The way we met, the circumstances were so odd. My grandfather, the fire, the story. I didn't know what all was going on. Until last night when I was sitting by his bedside, he woke up and was able to talk with me for a while. I wrote down some of what he said."

Moshe took a piece of paper out of his coat pocket and read a few of the words.

"Look," Moshe showed me, "the land set aside for the rebuild was fully paid for months ago. There is a deed to the land, to the new Center. He told me that the land was purchased in full, by the Lewis family.

"What?" I was shocked. "The Lewis family? That is the name of one of the suspects being prosecuted for the crime. Why would they do that? Their son was going to be convicted of burning down the Center. Why do they feel they need to help rebuild what their son destroyed?"

"It seems as though my grandfather had every intention of reopening the Center. He was even involved with the Lewis family."

"So why all the mystery and doubt? Why did he lead us to believe he would not reopen as if he was finished with the mission that he had worked on his whole life?" I asked.

"Hannah, I think he did it for you. For me. He saw something in you from the beginning. He knew it was time for you to find a deeper meaning in yourself. He wanted to stir something inside you. Wake you up, I guess."

"And you, Moshe?"

"He knew I was struggling with becoming a part of this community. I loved Israel and wanted to go back. I was planning to leave. In fact, I complained about it all the time.

After the Center burned down, I was so upset. I told him I was leaving. He was upset with me that I was abandoning my home, my family and my community. "

"So your grandfather was planning to continue the dream? The dream of a Center for the children and families to learn and grow and have community," Hannah said with a curled smile on her lips.

"There is more," said Moshe. "He left this for you." Moshe handed her a key.

"He said you would know what it meant."

I clutched it tight and remembered my dreams, my first meeting with Rabbi Marcus, the significance of what it all meant.

"As if he heard my thoughts again," Moshe said, "I know about your dreams, Hannah. I also had them for a while. That was when he brought me here, from Israel, from where I was studying in the yeshiva. A few years ago, my grandfather helped me figure out what my dreams meant."

"Those talks with him helped me find my way. My path in order to grow. The dreams also led me to you. I discovered that I also wanted to be a part of his mission. He wanted me to continue his work. At first, I wasn't sure that I wanted all this. The whole thing. It is such a big responsibility. Not just the Center but the learning, the Torah, the mitzvos, everything. It seemed like I was just going through the motions. It seemed like such a burden to take on. To serve God is a lot in itself, but to serve a whole community seems impossible.

"You were also moving away from your roots? Even though you seem so committed to Judaism?" I asked.

"Now that he is gone, I feel like I am so lost. What will I do without him? Should I let his dream die with him?

I could stay here for a while, I guess, and take care of my grandmother, I could make that my mission. But would I just be hiding from the real work I should be doing on myself?"

I was listening to his words and feeling sorry for his pain. I was also focused on the key in my hand. I knew what it meant. I knew it would unlock all the mystery. Moshe didn't know about the conversations I had with the rabbi; about the community, the fire, the destruction. He didn't know how the rabbi felt about the boy who started the fire or the whole truth about what happened that night.

The key would give me the answers I was waiting for. I was speechless for a moment. "I don't know what to say. I really loved your grandfather. He opened my eyes to myself. My searching, my dreams. That fire burning inside me all the time to find the truth in everything and everyone."

"Now I feel like I have realized something. Like the fire that had been burning all this time was inside me.

"I know certain things like it is time to move on from my job and my apartment in the City. I know that my family and my past do mean more to me than I admitted. But I still don't know what to do next."

"Your grandfather started me on a path, yes. But I am just at the beginning. He helped me look deeper at myself than I ever have before. And you, Moshe, you helped me to feel like I matter to myself, to my people, and to my community. Like I have a bigger reason for being here."

The words lingered a bit and then Moshe spoke.

"Hannah, will you be here when I get back?"

"I actually don't know, Moshe. I just don't know where I am headed."

"The deed said that the Center will reopen. We are not sure when at this point. The building plans are intact and underway and the money for the contractors was paid in full.

"I will be back from Israel soon. I feel that I must complete this part of my grandfather's dream."

"So what do you think will happen, Moshe? If you don't stay and continue to build your grandfathers dream?

"Do you think the Jewish community will survive? We are suffering a great loss right now. Bigger than the Center's burning. Like Rabbi Marcus told me a few days ago, it is not the books and the building burning that was the tragedy. It is the souls and lives of our children and our families that must not be destroyed along with it. You think that the Center will be reopened and people will start to come again?"

"I don't know. But I know that I plan to come back here and open a Jewish Center for the community as part of a tikkun (a fix) to the terrible flames that destroyed the first one.

"But I want to know Hannah, will you be here? Will you be there on the day we reopen? I want you to be by my side."

Have you ever made a decision that wasn't the right thing for you but you wanted to please someone else?

_____
_____
_____
_____
_____
_____
_____
_____
_____
_____
_____
_____
_____
_____
_____
_____
_____
_____
_____
_____
_____
_____
_____
_____
_____
_____
_____
_____

XII. The Return

Moshe would leave that night for Israel. Hannah returned to her small apartment. Now for some reason it seemed so small and cluttered. She started cleaning up and sorting piles of things that she no longer wanted.

It was a lonely evening and a time for her to come to terms with the rabbi's final request. Before she knew it she was on a train back to Brooklyn.

Avenue J was dark and the street lamp was out in front of the Marcus's home.

Hannah knocked slowly, out of respect, but knew no one would be home. They were all traveling to Israel. It seemed wrong to be in such a holy place all alone.

She walked down the long hallway and opened the door to the rabbi's office. A smile lit her face a bit as she noticed the strewn papers and pages of materials.

Papers of Yiddish, some Hebrew and English mixed. She remembered the time she had been here with him feeling awestruck by his glowing manner and at the same time a feeling of peace and warmth had surrounded her.

Hesitating a bit, she walked toward the desk. Now behind it. Moving the worn chair out of the way, not to sit on it. It seemed like an invasion of his very being.

Rabbi Marcus had studied in this office for more than 70 years. The chair was here, in this place, this sacred space, supporting him every moment of his life. He wrote sermons and words of Torah, speeches to recite under the chuppah for the bride and groom, birth stories for brit mila and simchat bat, bar and bat mitzvah wishes for the growing children and final prayers for the dying and mourning.

I stared at the floor knowing that I would find what I was looking for, I would find what I was searching for the very moment I placed my hand under the rug.

In one minute I would have the ending to my story. I would have everything I ever wanted. Everything I worked so hard for was at my fingertips.

I would have the truth. She took the key from her pocket.

Hannah lifted the rug and felt the floor board. Lifting the board as it creaked, she felt a metal box. She pulled it out and quickly found the key hole. She unlocked it and opened it up. The key was so shiny, so perfect. It could unlock even the most hidden parts of all of us.

There it was. Just as the rabbi told her. An envelope addressed to her. To Hannah Sloan of the New Yorker. Also nestled in the box was a small prayer book. It was just like her Bubby's. The one that she touched and felt close to all of these years. The one that she occasionally read from at her loneliest hours. And the one she had recently started looking at again.

At that moment Hannah opened it up and was frantically looking for that one prayer she had remembered from her dreams. The one about the master key. The one she could never reach in any of her dreams. The one that went up in flames each and every time.

Her movements stopped as she found the page. She began to say it over and over. As if through its words she would find her answers. Tears began to pour down her cheeks. She sobbed and sat there on the floor for a long time.

"Master of the World, Behold! I cast my prayer before You. For the Key of Life is in Your hand, and You have not transferred it to an agent."

Do you have a truth locked up deep inside of you? Whatever that secret is, do you wish to set it free? If so, how do you plan to do it? If not, how do you plan to live with it?

She placed the siddur, prayer book, back in the metal box and lifted the envelope. She slowly opened the sealed letter and took it from its home. She read...

***

Dear sweet, Chanele,

It has been a long journey for us together. So many talks and many good healthy arguments. (Hannah smiled as if the rabbi were right there next to her, ready for a fight.) You found the box and are about to read something that will give you many answers and leave behind even greater questions.

Please take the key that is beside the envelope. It is yours as a symbol of your quest to unlock the truth. It is a great quality in you and one you should continue to share with the world. Your desire to search for the truth and for what is right is holy and pure. When we met, I knew you would lead me on a personal journey of awakening. I knew when I saw you in my office as your eyes showed compassion for my pain. Your eyes shone with light as you saw my Moshe.

Your questions about the fire were so honest and I was not as honest with my answers. And I am sorry and hope you will forgive me.

(Hannah's tears dripped onto the pages.)

The night happened so fast, Chanele, I was in the study, as I told you. But that is not where I was before the fire started. I was tired and angry at the way the community was treating one another.

So much fighting between Jews - brothers and sisters. I was furious. I was scared and I was in terrible pain. I had stopped taking my pills. The ones you saw

Moshe bringing me the day we met. I thought I should feel the pain of the Holy One Blessed Be He. That I would share the suffering of Bnei Yisroel with Him.

Chanele, that night, the boy, Mathew Lewis, came to see me. I didn't have the time to give him. I didn't want to hear another one of his excuses for why he was failing school or why he couldn't find a job. He was a difficult child. He never fit into a box. But Mathew was a student of mine. He was a Jewish boy. A member of our community. I let him down. I let his parents down. I let God down.

That night, I ignored him. He wanted to talk to me. He looked so confused. Before I could reconsider my actions, there were flames everywhere.

I saw the flames begin to burn and I panicked. I ran to save the Torah. I removed it from the aron. I closed myself into my study and davened (prayed) and davened for the Jewish people. I davened for the Center. I davened for Mathew.

I started thinking it was meant to be. I believed that through this terrible fire, this terrible destruction, the klal, our people, would come together and bond over a common cause. I forgot to call the fire department, until it was too late. Then I started to choke and cough and collapsed to the ground.

I didn't press charges, because I believe it was my fault. I caused this pain and destruction. I was going to let it go and allow the pain of the community to subside without prosecuting the young boy. It didn't work that way. People wanted justice. Their version of justice. I am so sad that this young boy must suffer for my actions. His parents gave me the money to rebuild the Center, in his name. Maybe one day he will return to the community and find peace within its borders. Maybe he will return to a Jewish life.

I want the Center to reopen. I want Moshe to be in charge of its success. As I got to know you, Chanele, I thought perhaps he would rebuild, with you by his side. Chanele, thank you. Your quest for truth has caused me, an old man of 92 years old, to return. Your truth has awakened in me, my own teshuvah, return. Your dreams were true Chanele, your searching and your reaching hand has earned you the Key - The Master Key is the truth. And you have unlocked my truth - my Torah - into this world. Rejoice in the truth, Chanele, It is the only way to live.

***

Hannah closed up the letter and trembled and trembled.

Rabbi Marcus was a man of such compassion and wisdom. Why had he wanted to take so much blame for this terrible fire? In his way, he felt that he was helping the young boy.

Perhaps he was apologizing for not being there for him. I wasn't sure what to do with this information. I didn't want the world to know about the relationship the Rabbi had with Mathew Lewis. I just folded the letter and put it in my bag.

I placed the key in my bag as well, and left the room as I had found it. Dark, silent, yet warmed by its history. The tears had hardened on my cheeks and they were now cold and stiff. I wiped them away and closed the door behind me.

Have you ever kept a secret for a friend? Is there
something precious and powerful about a knowledge that
only you possess?

XIII.   The Pilgrimage

Six months later...

  Hannah had immersed herself in her search for truth and had flown to Israel to study in a women's seminary. Each day she would open her prayer book and embark on a spiritual journey of return.

  She had become well-versed in Hebrew and enjoyed studying the deepest ideas found in the Torah and Jewish texts. The tastes, sounds and feelings of the land of Israel had entered her core being. Her true Center.

  She was now burning to learn and grow in the power of the Torah.

  It was a Tuesday, Rosh Chodesh – the new month. She was on a walk now, not far from her quaint neighborhood in Jerusalem, to visit an old friend and teacher.

  So much time had passed that she resembled herself only in her physical appearance. Her soul and whole being – her neshama - had now taken on the lightness and likeness of a religious, spiritual and holy woman.

  She climbed the mountain slowly and pensively. She had walked these streets so many times over the past few months. With each step, her confidence and commitment to herself, her truth, was deepening.

  She was finally ready to own up to a truth that she was struggling with and uncertain about how to bring into the world. She arrived at the site she had set out for that day.

  Before her eyes settled on the destination, she let her gaze look out upon the beauty of the landscape. The history of the ground lay before her. The depth of the soil under her feet. She was excited and inspired at the same time. She was saddened at his passing. Too soon for her to truly learn from his wisdom.

She was at peace with what he did and how she handled his final words. She let her eyes rest upon the stone.

Rabbi Avraham Marcus
Husband, Father, Grandfather, Great-Grandfather
A Man of Truth, Wisdom and Warmth
1920-2012

Hannah knelt down and placed a stone upon the gravesite. She sat quietly for a while and then she spoke. "Rabbi, it is me, Hannah. Your friend. I know you are still watching over all of B'nei Yisroel. I feel your presence, even with me.

"I am sorry it has taken me a while to come and visit you. I have been studying our sacred texts. I feel that I am truly growing and understanding my place as a part of the Jewish people.

"I keep Shabbos for myself now and I am kosher. I even daven, pray, just like the way Moshe taught me. I use my siddur. The one you left me.

"It makes me feel warm and close to something great.

"I haven't had any dreams for a while now. Not since you passed away. My sleep is sound and peaceful and my days are awake and filled with enthusiasm. There is so much to learn and I am ready for it. My teachers are so inspiring. They are teaching me how to unlock my truth. I have something to give you."

She took a slip of paper from her bag. It was the letter he had written her. She also took out a book of matches. The matches were housed in a silver box that had an image of the holy temple in Jerusalem.

Hannah lit a match and she burned the letter. She placed the ashes upon the ground. At that moment it started to rain.

Not a heavy downpour. Just enough to burn out the flames and allow the smoke to rise quickly to the heavens.

"Water also brings us to a rebirth and renewal, Rabbi. You see? Not only does fire make way for us to rebuild, but so does the rain. Rain brings new life.

Hannah got up from her knees and as she turned around, there he was, standing alone and welcoming her. Moshe was standing there ready to take her home.

To return to the klal. To return to her family. To return to the Center.

There are some things that are reborn through destruction and others that are reborn through the waters of our tears and from the heavens. True teshuvah is a renewal and brings the waters of change. Is rebirth something you seek? If so, how do you plan to obtain it?

Epilogue: Shayndel's Journey and Further Prose

Personal Reflection as a means to Connection.

The following pages are additional journaling opportunities for you to think about. I have included some of my personal prose. Each piece represents a meaningful moment or time along my journey to personal change and a return to my truth. I look forward to hearing from you as well, along your journey. Please share your insights and inspirations with me.

May we continue to connect through my website at www.LiumiIsrael.com.

My Dream of the Matriarch, Leah

Author's Journey - A dream that has stayed with me and has recurred several times in my life is a dream of Leah. I use it to feel empathy and connect to the loss and pain of my sister's, both present and past. Leah, our matriarch, had a life of pain and loss as well as one filled with joy and love. Like many of us she, too, longed for something, something to make her feel complete.

What makes you feel complete?

My Story in a Dream

A few years ago I was blessed to have this dream. I had been married for a few months and was still uncertain and a bit frustrated about the traditional role of women in Judaism. It was an ongoing battle and one that I engaged in often. Sometimes it kept me up at night. And this night was no different.

At the time my husband and I were both studying in a yeshiva in Jerusalem and I was learning about our matriarchs, Rachel and Leah. Sisters and both married to the same man, our patriarch, Yaacov. Already I had a problem with this relationship.

Two women and one man. It seemed to contradict everything I hoped marriage would be. One man and one woman, together. Only desiring each other.

On another note, it couldn't possibly be fair to the women. Inevitably one of them, if not both, would suffer the pains of rejection and loneliness. It was Leah who felt the brunt of this triangle. She, the older and less desirable to her husband, seemed to be dealt the hand of isolation.

I empathized with her plight and often shed tears for what I was convinced was the male approach at love and the approval society allows them for the less-than-fair treatment of women. She got the short end of the stick.

I fell asleep angered and sad. I drifted into a sleep that was restless and tense.

This was the dream...

I was cold. I was alone and I appeared to be waiting for someone. I sat on a bench in a large room. It looked like a lobby in a museum or art gallery. In the distance a figure appeared - frail, petite and flowing in robes and scarves. She had long, medium-brown curly hair and fair eyes, almost translucent.

She approached me, took my hand and escorted me to an elevator located in the middle of the floor.

We entered and started descending farther and farther down. Not a word was said, but there was a familiar silence between us and I felt safe.

The door opened and we found ourselves in an auditorium with plush seating and velvet curtains. We sat together in the middle of the room and stared at the screen above our heads. The faces of our Jewish leaders flashed before our eyes.

Leaders; past, present and, perhaps, future. I noticed her face flash before me on the screen and only then knew who she was. She was Leah, our matriarch, my sister and she came to tell me something.

Slowly the seats that were surrounding us began to fill in with those very leaders I had seen on the screen in front of me. I was surrounded by them all and then everything went black and we found ourselves in the lobby once again. I was alone and I noticed Leah quickly approaching another elevator. I ran to her and she stopped, turned and took my hand. She was smiling and her eyes were filled with tears.

She entered the elevator - I wanted to go with her. I was overwhelmed by a feeling of urgency and despair at the thought of her leaving me. She shook her head, no.

It was cold. The doors closed behind her. I stood in silence and then I woke up. I had a wet tear rolling down my cheek. I felt refreshed and happy and at peace. I was silent for a while.

***

I thought about the dream for most of the day. I found myself staring ahead and was silent for a lot of the day. I wanted to keep my journey the night before hidden and secret. I wanted it to remain precious and special. It was clear that I had a just experienced a very real, very private moment with Leah.

I continued to learn about the women and their life. Now I felt a different sense of strength in myself and in her. She was happy with her life and with her role as a Jewish woman. She was a great Jewish leader, a devoted wife to her husband, a compassionate sister to Rachel and a loving and nurturing mother to her sons and the Jewish people.

I recount this dream often. It gives me strength and inspiration. It provides me with the extra bit of insight and understanding about my role as a Jewish woman.

Every Jewish woman is a leader and should be proud of her role as such. At times we need not trace our legacy back thousands of years. We can simply look in the mirror or at a photo album of our mothers and grandmothers. But at other times in life it is important and in fact necessary to remember the lives of our matriarchs and to relate to them on a more personal level.

When I light the Shabbat candles I always recite the following Blessing:

> **"In the spirit of Sara, Rivka, Rachel and Leah let Your light illuminate so that it be not extinguished forever and let Your countenance shine so that we are saved."**

When I go to sleep some nights I daven for her to return to me in a dream or a vision. I want to thank her for her wisdom and reassurance. I also just want to see her again like anyone would want to see a loved one who has passed away.

Thank you, Leah, my sister, for shaping my life as a woman and helping to define my role as a Jewish leader, wife and mother - today and forever.

Is there a woman in your life that you want to thank for strength and wisdom, reassurance and love?

_____
_____
_____
_____
_____
_____
_____
_____
_____
_____
_____
_____
_____
_____
_____
_____
_____
_____
_____
_____
_____
_____
_____
_____
_____
_____

Final Thoughts

Author's journey – A shower meditation (we must all have one, and if you don't get in the shower and create one, Now!) FYI - This shower was the size of my closet. If I can relax in that, you can relax in yours!

Shayndel's Shower Meditation:

How can I get the most out of this shower. These lukewarm, hard bullets of water dripping out of the spout, inside of a 2-foot space in the bathroom of my studio apartment. The shower is just inches from the toilet. I turned on the water, fast and hard, closed my eyes and washed away the reality of where I was. Cold and then hot water touched my skin. I allowed myself to imagine a tropical paradise somewhere in the Caribbean Islands. I was standing in a brisk waterfall off the cliff of a majestic mountain.

Secluded, isolated and very alone. The sounds of birds and the rustling of nature in the trees was all that could be heard for miles around. I took a breath, in came the steam of the heat, mixing with the cool air of the tropics. A rainforest. I was standing in a rainforest far away from the world that existed around me. As I let the water purge my skin I continued to fantasize about my private getaway and I allowed myself the pleasure of a clear mind and relaxed body.

Closing my eyes was the best part of the experience. I was truly able to escape into my dream, a new dream that I was controlling. Not the ones I had been forced into by my subconscious mind. No one else was invited into this dream. Just me and my rainforest and the sounds of endless time and space. The water felt soothing to my mind and body. I was able to release fears and tensions, and I was ready to emerge from the shower with clarity about myself and the next part of my journey. I turned off the shower and opened my eyes.

What are your shower meditations? See if you can come up with some.

_____
_____
_____
_____
_____
_____
_____
_____
_____
_____
_____
_____
_____
_____
_____
_____
_____
_____
_____
_____
_____
_____
_____
_____
_____
_____
_____

Excerpt from <u>My Father's Cup</u>

(Publication TBA)

Take a look at the following excerpt from my next novel, <u>My Father's Cup</u> (TBA). When writing the scene where Hannah returns home for Shabbos and her father made Kiddush that night in Brooklyn, I began to wonder - how far back do our memories and customs come from? Do we hold them as a precious part of our legacy? What can we do to keep them sacred, now and always?

Excerpt from <u>My Father's Cup</u>

(Publication TBA)

Holocaust - 1939

I looked at Miriam just 6 years old. She did not understand what was happening. How could she? All she knew was helping Mama and playing with her friends. We entered the building slowly. We got inside, the smells were familiar, but the sites were foreign. Cousin Moshe was smiling although I could see he was as nervous as we were. When the doors opened we saw a bright blue sign on the door. "Welcome home, Labele and Miriam."
Cousin Moshe opened the door. He knocked twice like Tatti used to do.

Inside the apartment it continued to smell like home. Not this new home but our old home. Warm bread, cakes and kugels, chicken and brisket. I hadn't realized what day of the week it was. It was Friday, Erev Shabbos. We hadn't had Shabbos in so long.

My cousin Moshe and his wife Faige settled us into our room. And our cousins, Yosef and Chaim, were there to help us as well. They all seemed so nice and concerned about us. It will be nice to spend time with them until after the war when we return to our home in Poland. When Mama sends for us. I am sure Tatti will be back from the work camp they sent him, and the other strong men to as well. "Children," we hear Cousin Faige yell from downstairs. "Father will be home soon from Shul. Come to the table."

Miriam and I notice a pretty yellow dress on her bed and a suit for me to wear for Shabbos. We dress quickly and join the others downstairs. Before we join them I gently unwrap the silver cup. I had it clutched to my chest for the journey. It has seen me through the journey and made it to the other side. A few times I almost sold it for a warm morsel of food or a warm blanket for Miriam and myself.

But she forbade me to do it. I remember clearly, as we boarded the train, Mama said I would know what to do with it when the time came. "She did not mean for you to sell it, Labele," urged Miriam. "I know Mama did not mean that." I clutched it once again to my chest and raced down the stairs.

As we enter the formal dining room, Cousin Faige noticed the cup. "How beautiful," she said. "Quickly, give it to me and I will shine it for Shabbos." You can use it to make kiddush with Cousin Moshe. Me? I should make kiddush with my Tatti's cup?

He did.

But no "Amen" from Mama... The silence afterward would haunt me forever.

"May our lives be filled to the top with the sweetness of Shabbos," I exclaimed.

Can you recount your last Shabbos experience? How old were you? Who did you spend it with? What Shabbos experience has stayed with you?

_____

_____

_____

_____

_____

_____

_____

_____

_____

_____

_____

_____

_____

_____

_____

_____

_____

_____

_____

_____

_____

_____

_____

_____

_____

_____

_____

_____

So, my sister, we have come to the end of our short journey together. I know we will continue on our way. Perhaps finding each other again. But until then, may you be blessed to continue to find meaningful moments and continue to make all of your moments meaningful. Remember, memory is the protagonist of our lives.

With love and sisterhood,

Shayndel